WYNN: THE LIFE OF A PROLETARIAN PUSHED FROM PILLAR TO POST (1948-1976)

(A FRAGMENTED BLACK COMEDY)

BY

EVAN GWYN WILLIAMS

TUBA PRESS

GREAT BRITAIN

First published 2007

By Tuba Press
Tunley Cottage, Tunley,
Nr. Cirencester,
Glos GL7 6LW
Great Britain

Typesetting & printing
By Tuba Press

British Library Cataloguing-in-Publication Data.
A catalogue record for this book is available
from the British Library.

ISBN 9780907155607

CONTENTS

Previous Books By The Same Author Include
'The White Balloon & Other Poems' 78 pages Tuba Press 1998, And The Two Reviewed Below.

Mammon
Tuba Press, £18.00

Evan Gwyn Williams's magnum opus, *Mammon,* written after he was evacuated from Saudi Arabia during the Gulf War, is a scathing critique of our war-mongering, money-grubbing consumerist society. It is Jeff Nuttall's Bomb Culture meets Howl meets The Waste Land meets Marx.

... I walk
athritic (sic) and longing for home
bored with tears that glue my eyes,
to the sea & the destroyed fast food shops
the mined beach the machine gun nests
the slogans on the walls

WE LOVE BUSH
WE LOVE THATCHER

("Apostrophe to Agamemnon")

CLARE POWELL (Planet Magazine 169)

Evan Gwyn Williams CELEBRATION AND DEATH OF SUSAN CONSTANCE (1944-1997) /TUBA PRESS /Tunley Cottage, Tunley, Nr. Cirencester. Glos. GL7 6LW / 63pp / £6.00/ ISBN 0 907155 45 6 .

An honesty of feeling is conveyed in CELEBRATION AND DEATH OF SUSAN CONSTANCE as Evan Gwyn Williams brings together over 90 sonnets in nine threnodies or laments. The reader cannot help but notice the control and sincerity which the poet brings to these poems;

Eyes dark and luminous without the shadow of death
And out of the trees the sound, suddenly of leaves:
A hint of renewal - blood on the torn sleeve.

(XI-NINTH THRENODY)

BYRON BEYNON

INTRODUCTION

(The characters in this script are entirely fictional
and resemble no one. Place names do not exist
except on scientific maps. The only reality
is memory which, in any case, falsifies events.)

In 1956 the World War was over by 10 years. Immediately after the electorate gave the mandate for socialism. Steel, coal and railways were nationalised and the road transport system. The aristocracy and the capitalist Class was absolutely furious and directed its bile at the Soviet Union. McCarthyism permeated the Western World. Hundreds of thousands of soldiers and Airmen were stationed in Germany, (e.g. RAF Borgentreich,) to front up to the communists. Liverpool Street Station, London was crammed with military Personnel on the platforms and over the bridges shrouded in steam from the locomotives, in preparation for what seemed another war. The relations with the German population not yet de-Nazified around these camps was filled with tension often erupting into violence and murder.

* * *

We not only lead political lives we lead emotional lives. We move in a political mores while half-crazed with sex-hormones and the need to reproduce, to love and be loved. Also half-crazed women are everywhere, their unhappiness and confusion is a dramatic set piece. Girls cry: are insecure and downright awkward, holed up in flats and bed sits having observed their parent's failure. Memory is a dramatic interlude fuelled by crisis.

* * *

MEMORY is the DRIVING FORCE

of

MISERY 'n' the BLUES

Memory fragments the consciousness while searching for futile answers to futile questions because we are searching for our identity amid a thousand Masks in the theatre of life where the lights are dimmed and the sound system is closed down as the phantoms flee into the recesses of one dimensional space.

In one moment, childhood and the misery of adulthood, can be fused in split seconds of memory. Why would a person screw a horse in a ruin in a remote valley. Rural life is full of such incidents of buggery. Urban life cramped and without charm. The political world of cruelty awaits the innocent child who is unaware of time, absorbed in childish self in the railway Embankments or in the barracks on the undulating German plains of wheat.

TIME is the ARTIST of DESTINY
MEMORY is the MASTER TIME

* * *

In the psychiatric hospitals the stricken mentally ill are abused and maligned. They are the 'victims of an Unjust God yet are without sin and Jesus is their Saviour although he has abandoned them. They are helpless, lobotomised, and experimented on by a medical establishment with no conscience whatsoever.
They are given drugs with Parkinsonian side effects. They drag one leg and tremble like leaves blown on a tree. Electric shocks are sent through their brains while they gag on mouthpieces or get up and drive their thigh bone through the hip socket: given hormones while they grow long eyelashes and flutter their eyelids at their developing breasts, scalded in hot water while blind from syphilis. Many are casualties of war, especially displaced Poles and Jews.

* * *

We live in an world of uncertain where others have shown the way. Great Artists have come and gone. We pick up their instruments, the trombone and saxophone and are found to be wanting. God has tricked us. We are looking through the camera lens but see nothing but despair: and here is the paradox. It is all so hilarious. It is so funny it brings tears to your eyes.

MEMORY is FRAUDULENT
DESIRE of FULFILMENT a DECEPTION

Nature is beautiful: the sea is beautiful. Birdsong.
Wind in the leaves or sun
In the branches of a tree is beyond all misery.

The sunlight surfaces of the sea on the continental shelves hide the terrible sunless depths where hardly anything lives. This surface area consists of half the Globe and is impenetrable. There are no tides and no currents only a silent cold stillness.

* * *

In the realm of time Radical Feminism got a grip on the already psychopathic personalities of certain women — all things sugar and spice has passed into myth. There is no doubt that so-called women are incapable of love. It's just not in 'em. Writers as Valerie Solanus and Germaine Greer, were heaven sent to the Female sociopath These writers legitimised their sick vision of reality, of women's role in society! The political situation was that trades unions had infiltrated the Labour Party and their education was Marxist. Class struggle intensified, but radical Feminists saw the working class push for power as a domain of Chauvinist Pigs and Sexists. Marriages fell apart with "irretrievable breakdown." laws.

Distortion of reality by indiscriminate use of language took the form of *cynicism*. To Germaine Greer and others men are quite simply beasts, not only beasts but Nazis, violent, brutal, repressive and beyond redemption. Men are incapable Of love, despite hundreds of thousands living until death do us part. Men distort Reality. They rape indiscriminately and in marriage, too. Marriage is therefore illegitimate. We live in a distortion of reality, a two tier philosophical limbo where.

CYNICISM RULES OK

In Radical Feminism the man-hater is born again. The radical feminist is ugly with excessive body hair and mephitic whiff, bony kneed, excessively muscled, with dry split hair, anti-Christian, and Hellish. Rejected by men as ugly they seek primitive and unconditional revenge. The Radical Feminist is born into Misery through the WEAK FATHER who fails to teach them the meaning of love, but it goes even deeper than this. It is religious. The sick radical feminist has been rejected by God, maker of all things, who deformed her and made her ugly. The misery of betrayed female must be avenged. Hell hath no Fury like a Woman Scorned. She must also malign his son hung on a cross, having a son to save mankind is an insult since no one suffers like the ugly woman. She is denied everything under the sun.

HATRED AND MISERY is the MODE of EXISTENCE
And
EMOTIONAL CHAOS a WEAPON

Woman have orgasms. They pursue a double morality. They invent the insult. Men are impotent. The femme fatale is a shadow on a screen. The Amazon is re-invented. They are not sex objects, nor midwives of the moon. They alone look into the Eye of the Womb. They shave their heads like convicts and cry sisterhood. The moon looks on with a smile on its face over the tides which rise and fall over the hostile globe where Aphrodite was born with Eros at her side in the nightmare of existence.

* * *

In the Psychiatric hospitals the deformed children of thalidomide lay in their urine and shiver. They are without mothers who have fled at the horror of the womb. Who is to blame but God who is the holy father, a patriarch who rules through cruelty. An eye for an eye and a tooth for a tooth.

* * *

There is a box in a flat in Sybil's room. No one knows how it got there and it is not mentioned in the text but Wynn opened this box and read terrible and nauseating things. It seemed to be in the form a diary maybe written by Sybil but it was not in Sybil's hand writing, also the box had a frog's skin pierced by pins. The box held secrets but when Wynn returned to explore the contents a little more it had gone. And that was the day there was a terrible storm, one of those summer storms when there was a dreadful moan coming from somewhere and crows were blown against the window as though they had lost their way.

* * *

In Borgentreich, a British Camp on the foot hills of the Hartz mountains Airman banged the mess hall tables with knives and forks until the C.O came and gave them a lecture on the consequences of mutiny. In the far East after the war the establishment wanted to retain service men to fight the communists and faced mutinous troops. The establishment had to back down.

Feminism distorts reality by asserting ideas contrary to female physiology, biology and psychology In other words feminism distorts the truth. Feminist writers spawned out of bourgeois academies are psychopaths, childless lesbians with father complexes living in the shadows of Plato's cave. Feminists lack experience of labour exploitation because they are physically weak and ineffective. They are reactionary and conservative. And so contributed to the destruction of socialism. Their goddess is Margaret Thatcher who put the barbed wire around Rhigos Halt and wrote the sign *Trespassers will be prosecuted.* Ann with her tea cosy hat is dead.

During the era 1948 to 1979 Britain was a socialist state. Hitchhikers were everywhere riding the BRS trucks. Forces personnel did not pay for tickets on the railways. They were let through for free along the Wye Valley and the Severn Bore. That world has gone forever into the network of memory. The ruling class has reasserted its will in the form of Thatcherism. Insult piled on insult.

Radical feminism is seen for what it is, put quite simply, rubbish. They deny their own gender. They unrelentingly harp on negative aspects of life. . Women are harpies, sluts, harridans, bits of fluff, whores, bags, scrubbers, birds, bitches, bits of crumpet. And they menstruate. How hideous!

O horror of Menstruation! Horror! Odour!
Et cetera Nature is a load of bunk!
Are we mad? Are we victims of dolour?
Better be without it and lay among flowers.

There is an allegory of the ugly woman, so ugly as to be grotesque who made rude jokes: had warts and yellow teeth, coarse, hairy skin and was fat. However, the ugly woman was wise and knew that women needed power to control men and to be thought of as clever and sensitive to others needs. An educated and refined man was tricked into marrying her, tricked by a spell and enchantment, but, in fact, her ugliness was a disguise for she turned out to be beautiful like Heddy Lamar.

Sybil is none of these for she does not exist except in imagination, or *phantasia*. She is distant from tactile sensation, the "here and now" of sensation: she is absent from external senses. She is the *femme fatale* of shadow and celluloid or like the soldiers shrouded in light and steam on the platforms of time and history. But she did lead Wynn into the caverns of hell like Eurydice led Orpheus into the realm of Hades.

The Castle of Flowers has withered at the root
The scent turned sour
Time hardly moves in the cold shadow
Of the dial, passing the hour.

All that is mysterious darkens, light
Struggles in the flower, white on white.

Who now has the box of horrors. Who dares look into the future which is all of past. Mass movements come and go into the collective wisdom. Are we wiser? An ideal world awaits free of the shadows of Plato's cave. Dare we build more castles in the air?

Ebenezer Chapel

July 2005

Ann

1

Garden of Eden where grief strode sulking
viewed the fields of gorse and grass . . .
I see you in your garden, Ann, beloved of God's
creatures, raised in summer heat.
You were the Harpie, strange old crone,
in a tea cozy hat. The wireless
lay still on the table like a face,
dismal as the rain on your window.
Ann, you stood on the Halt waiting for the train,
eggs laid in washed cloth, ghost of a ghost
of Hamlet's mother not knowing a dead son.
Progress took your eyes away. You watched
the hills. Blindly, too, I watched hands,
like roots of trees, at the fire's flames.

2

Claudius poured poison in a king's ear -
the river ran through the Halt to eternity.
Ann, with wizened ear to the wireless
heard all, queen of her humble dwelling
with only a son's ghost at her side.
The river runs on from hills, over stones
over drifting wood and leaves of autumn,
over limestone and silica - blood in the veins,
cooling liver, kidney's stink.
Now Ann has gone to blissful heaven
who walked with mother to church three miles
through summer heat, and frosty christmasses.
Summoned by God's only son she listens
for hers - the womb's dry seed.

1

BORGENTREICH: 1959

The Camp

The blue flannel uniform chafed his legs. It was hot over the undulating fields. There were no hedgerows as in England and no mountains either. Along the roads you sometime came to a wooden cross on which a figure of Christ hung. He took the uniform off and lay on the bed and watched the summer flies circling the ceiling. Four airman occupied the room usually, but there was only one there at the moment, and he lay snoring. Eventually, he took up a novel and began to read until the snoring got on his nerves so he went outside and lay on the grass looking up at the cloudless sky. Further down the path the Yanks were drilling. He'd never seen anything like it. They seemed to be all chewing gum with their hats on the sides of their heads like a bunch of comics out of a movie.

He lay there in the sunlight for awhile and remembered the little German and his buxom wife who'd showed him, and a few other airmen, what seemed original photographs of concentration camp inmates, and that was in Warburg. He still could n't get over how they'd giggled, drunkenly, over them. All he was interested in was getting his hand up the woman's drunken skirt. Then there was the time he'd woken up in the middle of Borgentreich pissed in a small haystackwith a German farmer looking straight down on him, and then...and then he fell asleep in the sun. He woke up not feeling too good and went down to the mess and ate bacon egg and chips.

"The Yanks won't eat English grub," said a cook, "we're gettin' a whole lot o' steaks in an' corn cobs."

"Christ," exclaimed another, "we'll be eatin' like kings."

"One of the blacks poured rice puddin' over his Lancashire Hotpot," lamented a gaunt, pimply youth.

Outside the sky was still cloudless.

He walked back to the billet passed the trucks that were lined up in case the Russians invaded. It was all so unreal.

When he got back to the billet the other blokes were laying on their beds exhausted after their shifts. He did n't like any of them. And that was what forces life was like. No-one liked anyone. Eveyone suffered.

One of the cooks was a lifer, that meant twelve years of sweatin' over fried eggs and chips." He was a North Walian who mimed masturbation by beating his groin with his fist in a vast sweeping action, and giggling through loose fitting dentures. His face was always covered in a thin gauze of sweat.

The other bloke had receding curly ginger hair with pale skin. He came from Blackpool. He was begrudgingly doing his national service, never drank nor smoked, and put money away every week. He said little but managed to convey an attitude of disgust about eveything and everyone. While the North Walian slept in his underpants, ginger slept in a pair of pyjamas his mother sent him once a fortnight. She must've kept a bed and breakfast.

The third bloke was a half-pint with a hooked nose from Mansfield who viewed the world with a permanent ironic smile. It was rare to have the four of them at one time in the billet.

"I saw the Yanks drilling today," he said.

"Bledy shower, Taff," said ginger.
"The commies must be really scared," said the half-pint.

Outside the sky was still cloudless. He went down to the NAAFI to get his BAFS changed into Deutsch Marks, bought a couple of packs of duty free fags and walked into the German village. The village had about five Gasthofs, but only one or two was used by the troops, the others were hostile. These people were Hitler's Deutscher Volk, pure bred German peasant stock, the oompah! oompah! Rosen Montag non-fraternization brigade. He did n't like 'em. Funny thing, though, he liked the German soldiers on the camp. They smelled of shampoo, and wore tailor-made gabadine unforms, and had immaculate manners, but the Deutcher Volk were gross, red-faced, stupid pigs. He sat in the Gasthof and ordered a bier with schnapps. He had noticed, too, how clean the Germans were. Every glass of bier was washed, every table polished, the floors, too. He sat there amid all this cleanliness and drank until the alcohol numbed his senses, thinking of the spit and sawdust mining pubs of his hometown.

"How's it goin' Taff," said a voice, and a fat bloke sat next to him, "how many days to do?"

"Seven," he said.

"I would n't get into any trouble. These Krauts are all steamed up I can tell. I'm goin' in a few days myself."

Outside the sky was still cloudless.

They ate marinated pork chops together and talked about the the brothels in Hanover, and the bloody cold war, and these Nazi-lovin' bastards. Time went by. They drank some more.

"Let's go," said the fat bloke, "and do a last round."

"OK"

They visited the out of bounds joints but since they were out of bounds there were hardly anyone in them anyway. The sullen barman seemed almost glad to see them. Outside it got dark. Eventually, they went back to the original Gasthof. It was full now,with airman, and the back room full with boistrous Germans. There were women there, too. The two men sat at the tables watching, drinking, waiting.

“That dame’s hot,” said the fatman, “ her husband's gone on a course to England.”

Wynn asked her to dance. She came up close. He could smell her hair, and feel the movement of her hips and belly against his. And he pressed his swelling genitals against her.

“Would you like to get some fresh air,” he asked.

“Yes,” she said, “in a while,” she sat down, making him sweat out his desire.

Suddenly a bier mat hit him on the side of the head and spun onto the table, scrawled on the back was “Heil Hitler.” The fat signalman put his hand on his friend’s sleeve.

“I would n’t do anything if I was you, Wynn, in seven days you’ll be on the boat back to blighty. Know what I mean.”

The Germans let go a chorus of raucous mocking laughter. The English woman gazed at him across the space of the dancefloor.

“Let’s go,” he said to the fatman.

Out of the Gasthofs tumbled the airmen, watched by a solitary German policeman with a large dog at his side. The night was warm and cloudless with a hint of farm dung in the air, dung and straw. The dog sniffed and the policeman figited in his hot uniform. The airmen formed groups along the winding road, talking, laughing, fired by bier and schnapps in the heat and fragrance of the undulating summer fields that stretched into the distance.

"Hear that, Taff," said the fatman, "something's happened."

There was a muffled bang.

"Maybe not," he replied.

When he got back to the billet he fell on the bed in his clothes and woke up in the early hours, chilled,with a hangover.

A couple of days later he heard the shots of a funeral salute. Someone had been killed on the road a few nights back. An airman had lurched in front of a car as it moved through the crowds, accelerating at the edge. A deep silence fell over the camp, the sky clouded over and a cold wind blew over the fields.

A couple of days later he was gone.

Funny thing, he could not recall, in any detail, his leaving the camp. Nor the journey across the German plains, nor crossing the channel in the damn boat. The memory was gone for ever.

———0o0———

2

EROS AND APHRODITE

"There is no unity left, no wholeness."
(Ernst Fischer)

1

He lay beside her on the small bed. She was crying. She was always crying, mostly about her mother and father. Also she had a boy friend at sea, some sort of mate or other. She cried about him, too, because her mother did n't want her to marry him.

She was tormented and so she tormented him.

"Wynn," she said, "I like you, but I don't think I love you."

"Do you love John?" he asked. John was the seaman.

"He's nice," she said.

What the hell did she mean by that? He rolled her over, and entered her. She had good breasts, very good breasts, and wide hips. And she liked it, but was always holding something back no matter how often they did it together. Consequently, they pretended they enjoyed it. It was all a game anyhow, a game they were both loosing because they did n't know the rules. And the rules were that you had to give everything without regret, and in giving only half she gave nothing.

Next day he met her at the university and took her to the station. She wore a blue costume with a white scarf. She looked absolutely lovely. He kissed her in the carriage and left. And stood waving on the platform as the train pulled out. And that was the last time they made love because when she returned she rejected him. It was very painful, but he left the city, and so avoided any embarrassment.

2

The sea stretched out before him in aqua-marine, opal and green. The hills in the distance were purple and light blue stained by the sun and patched by the passing clouds. Everyday you looked out they were different. At night moonbeams ran down into the sea on which his angels trod and disappeared as the night clouds moved and the stars peeked down from the constellations.

In the college common room anarchists sat and scowled at the communists. The christians stood apart and aloof. Those without any convictions dreamed of the future where there was nothing but the tranquility of the sea outside.

And at the end of the term there was a dance, and he wrote to her asking if she'd like to come, but she declined. And that was the last he heard from her. And he felt regret for past.

*   *   *

He lay between the blonde's legs in the bed, but could n't concentrate on the job since her mother was in the other room.

"I can't," he said, "what about your mother?"

Rain hit the windowpane. She did n't care about her mother. In any case the rooms were divided by thick Welsh granite. Next

Saturday they planned to go to the Lleyn for a dirty weekend but she did n't turn up. She'd got married instead.

Time went by.

The sea stretched before him in aqua-marine, and green. The hills in the distance were purple and metal blue, stained by the sun and passing clouds.

* * *

He lay in SW 15 in a bedsit. The gas fire spluttered. He turned the dark haired girl over, but she just lay there indifferently. She was pregnant by a postgraduate. She was to enter hospital. It was all arranged by the landlord. She lay in the hospital, crying, with a scar across her. Much later he heard she was in Singapore.

He went to work on an 88 bus through Vauxhall, and passed the Tate Gallery into the West End and lay in the bath of the Salvation Army at lunch break. On the bus he read *"The State and Revolution"* the Communist Party had given him. Then he met a girl with a moustache and made love to her in Earl's Court. She cried all the time and lay rigid on the floor. And for some inexplicable reason they got married and moved to a sea side town. In the sea side town the ships cut black shadows on the horizon. The sea was drab and lifeless. The marriage lasted seven years and there was a little girl. In the marriage he was passive. He worked. He came home. He watched the black and white television. (He liked Alf Garnett.) He did a correspondence course. He wrote poems in rhyme. He played chess and threw the board out of the window in frustration and his wife was appalled. They went to the theatre and got to know the actors. They went to the West Country to her aunt's farm. They made love in bed, on the floor and behind a mountain wall. They visited the five valleys. He was searching for something but he did n't know what except mining disasters. And she got restless and bored and angry. Still he was passive, tormented by demons. His soul was passive, chained in a dungeon so abstract it did not exist except in his bleak imagination. Suddenly the whole-thing exploded, and he found himself alone in a bedsit. Broke.

* * *

He sat in the stores reading an engineering drawing. His insides were knotted up. He felt tense and moody. He was in the dungeon and with him was a girl, but it was n't his wife it was the one who'd rejected him. They lay in the dungeon with candles flickering to the plaintive sound of the trumpet of Miles Davies, and his soul was at rest. Was this what life was about, he thought, this torment, this rest? He'd made a mistake. He'd have to learn to live with it like everybody else. He went home and looked at his wife. She was repulsive. He picked up his daughter and kissed her. She was not repulsive. She had a turned up nose and freckles. She was two years of age. But his wife was repulsive. She was a beast, and a devil as far as he was concerned.

And time went by.

And time resolved the matter for she turned her feminine ire on him in the form of an organized attack. She joined the feminist movement, and the language of invective and of insult entered the household. "You're a sick fuckin' bitch," he said.

"Sick! No-one is more sick than you, you drunken chauvinist pig. What d'you want me to do, sit around and knit?"

"Sit around and knit?"

"Oh, what do you understand?"

"Understand?"

"Stop repeating what I'm saying, will you!"

"I'm repeating what you're saying because I can't believe my ears. What's 'sit and knit' mean?"

"You want me to be a passive little wife, that's what it means."

"Passive?"

"There you go, again."

"Oh, hell, I've got enough problems."

"Problems? Your problems have just started. What are these then?"

"Calender pin-ups. I got them from the nut and bolt salesman. He gives calenders out."

"Disgusting. I feel insulted!"

"Insulted?"

"Aw shaddup!"

And she went into the bedroom which seemed to hang above the high street and sobbed pitifully. Over the bay the sun went down as the ships cut holes in the horizon. What misery! What had he done to deserve this! It had all started a long time ago he was sure. Everything he had observed and done had come to this confrontation. Maybe he'd taken the wrong turning on the road, but where was the road leading? He looked out of the window. The streets were empty, and wet, and the sun was down behind the clouds. Another day was over. Another daywas done and he was no closer his destiny, if he had one.

He sat down in a chair and smoked a fag. There was no sound from the bedroom only the wind in the eaves moaning its lament. Later he went to bed, and lay looking at the ceiling, at the shadows from the street lights and an occasional passing car. And fell asleep until he was awoken by a shout.

----0o0----

3

TEN FRAGMENTS

1.

They were in the hills in an old derelict farmhouse in which the wind whined. There was Tal Jones holding the horse, and Aneurin Thomas stood on a stone fuckin' the horse. In/out In/out. Aneurin had a well formed dick.

"Do you want a go, Wynn," he asked.

"No, you carry on," he replied.

And the sun started to go down over the hills.

2.

He came home from the psychiatric hospital reading books on psychosis and neurosis. It was summer the air was clean and fresh. The wind was in the trees outside. He took up a piece of paper and wrote a poem. And that was his first poem.

3.

They lay in a cave in West Wales around a wooden fire they had built hearing the waves beat against the rocks. Pugh was playing his guitar, light from the fire flickering over his face. The girl lay her head full of blonde curls on Wynn's chest. Over the sea the moon hung like a coin.

4

He fed the spastic black kid. Food fell down his jaw. He wiped thc kid clean. When he'd finished he went back to his original ward. It was winter. The coal fire burned in the grate. An old man shouted from his cot.

"Shoot he fuckin' lot o' 'em. Nurses. Doctors. The fuckin lot."

And time went by as before. And thc fire crackled and the molecules broke down to ashes.

5

And it was because of Pugh that he came to the sea side town. He had visited Pugh there when Pugh was an Art student. And he liked the atmosphere of the town and the relaxed manner the students. The sea side town was Castell Blodau. And he got a job there on the docks in Castell Blodau and this was about 1968. And he was on a kind of journey, but he did n't know it at the time. And although time went by he did n't take much notice of it because of the journey and he was looking for something on that journey but he did n't know what. All the time he sat in the stores of the dock he longed for this other girl with her blue costume and her white scarf.

6

They were on the Red & White bus going up to see his mother in the council house. The bus bounced along the valleys, along the terraced streets and the pits. He was very proud of her being at the university and all, and he felt very warm toward her. That anxiety he felt when he was alone had subsided because she had began to share his dreams. He was her poet and when they got to the village his mother got out her best crockery, and had a friend in. They all had tea together, and Joy gave his mother a little plant which his mother put on the windowsill. And that was the first and last time his mother saw Joy. And time went by as before.

7

His father was carrying in the coal. He worked with a great deal of concentration wheeling in the black glistening stuff to the coal house.

“Help your father,” said his mother.

But his father did n’t need help. When Wynn tried to pick up some coal his father said: “leave that!” and so leave it he did. Besides, he was in love with Hilary Finch who was not in love with him. She seemed to like Dai ‘Dick’ Evans who was Rugby Evan’s brother. He cried about her once or twice in the council house outside toilet among the cobwebs and spiders.

“What you doin’ in that bloody toilet,” shouted his mother, “watch that whitewash on your school uniform!” He was in the grammar school and had a navy blue uniform with *“Straight as an Arrow from the Bow,”* in Welsh as a motto. He stopped snivelling and looked at his uniform. Sure enough there was whitewash on it.

“Fuckin’ Hilary Finch,” he moaned.

Now that his father had nearly finished carryin’ in the coal he noticed how proud he was at stackin’ up the wall with every lump locked into position. He thought his father might’ve been workin’ on a farm at sometime, and had maybe built stone walls. Who knows? Anyhow it was summer so he went off to the farm to help with the hay. The hay smelt like hay usually did, musty and sweet, a lovely warm aroma. He picked the hay up onto the gambo with a pitch fork and hay seeds fell on his hair and face. And later he drank some cider from a barrel the farmer gave them. And they unloaded the hay in the barn with the dray horse swishing its tail, being bitten by gadflies and hornets. How disgusting Aneurin Thomas fuckin' a horse, he thought, and wondered what it felt like and into his reverie came the farmer who had a red face and a moustache like Hitler with a wet Craven 'A' fag wagging under it. (He was always drinking water for his bad kidneys and had a flat chested wife like a stick insect.) And the farmer gave him two shillings and sixpence for helping with the hay. And he went home down the track past the little river that made its song over its myriad stones making its unique music.

And time went by as before.

8

His father was slappin' him round the head, tears flooded down his face. "Find the fuckin' money," said his father, gritting his false teeth who was plenty mad. Wynn grubbed around in the wet grass, but could n't find any. "You lost my fag money," said his father bitterly. His father went two days without fags. And Wynn developed a hatred for his father that would never quite go away.

9

Wynn was in Bexley Heath. Joy gave him beer from the booze cabinet of the detached suburban house. His father was dead and he never thought about the camp. Joy was sitting on the floor so he slid his hand under her skirt and stroked her bare thigh. He looked out of the window and saw it was getting dark. " I feel a sense of loss when the darkness comes down," he said. Later, he went back to London with the picture of her family in his heart. Her father who did a disappearing act and her mother who loved Jesus more than her husband. And that was why the girl kept on weeping. Or had she invented a situation in which she felt safe weeping. You never can tell, he thought because people lie all the time, even to themselves.

10

Wynn stood on Glynneath square. Well, it wasn't a square, really, it was just that the buses stopped there among a couple of shops. He had just walked up from the Miner's Welfare Cinema. His father had meant to meet him there, but did n't turn up so he went to PontWalby to his Aunty Maggie May. He liked his Aunty Maggie May because she was kind to him, and she giggled a lot. However, she was ill and in bed. She had 'water' everybody said. Neither did she have any children.

When he got to his Aunty Maggie May's his mother said: "where's your father?" "I dunno," he answered. "You wassupposed to meet him on the square," she said. His Aunty Maggie May giggled. His mother gasped. Much later his father appeared. He said: "I walked all the way up the Glynneath Bank to the Halt for the bugger, and he was here all the time." His Aunt giggled. His mother gasped, and his Uncle Shonni who had a speech defect said: "I'll give the bugger a fourpenny." That night Wynn rolled around on the floor with a huge teddy bear Maggie May kept in the bedroom. He punched it. He jumped on it, and fell asleep beside it. He was happy, but could n't figure out why his father walked ten miles to look for him all the way up the bank, and to the Halt, then all the way back to Glynneath and in the dark as well.

And the days of his childhood went by.

———0o0———

4

THE MOON AND THE DEMENTED

He was in Hirwaun Band Room, soaking wet. He'd walked two and a half miles through bitter Autumn rain with his new trombone. The band Room was the winding shed of an old disused, pit, or, in any case, it looked like a winding shed. In the corner of the winding shed was another little shed, a shed within a shed. And in the little shed there was a bucket in which the bandsmen took a piss. The bucket stank of stale urine.

"Play any note," said his friend who was only eighteen, "an' I'll tell you what the next note is."

He blew a note, then he blew another note.

"That last note is A," he said.

Wynn was amazed. "How d'you know that," he said.

"I got perfect pitch," said the kid.

When the other bandsmen got there the leader took Wynn's trombone and blew his part because Wynn could n't read music that well. He could recognize the notes but had no idea about rhythm. He was rhythmically daft. So he played by ear. Hit or miss, mostly miss. He was twenty two years of age, and lost in a world of make believe music. After the band finished he went home miserable and alone. The kid's name was Robert Jones. Wynn thought the kid was a genius.

Wynn sat in the kitchen with his mother. He thought, I can't go on like this, and put on a Louis Armstrong record. In a while he got a job in a psychiatric hospital in Talgarth. Everyone was friendly. All the nutters stared at him. There was Big Freddie, lobotomized who went around all day saying Krushchev ought to be dead and MacMillan. There was Alfie who sang Abide with Me, and all the Polish soldiers who stared into space. A couple of months passed and he got a transfer to Cardiff. Robert Jones went to the Royal Academy of Music. Wynn swapped his trombone for an alto sax and imagined himself to be Charlie Parker, rhythmicallydaft. But somehow he learned to read music. He was improving all the time. But one day he went out and sold his sax and gave the whole damn thing up. He came in one night to the admission ward when all the patients were asleep. There was a fat, young married nurse laying across two chairs.

"How about a cup of tea?" he asked. He followed her to the kitchen and she turned from the boiling kettle: leaned back against the wall as women do and stared at him. He closed with her and kissed her open mouth as he pressed his thigh against her crotch. It was then she wiggled her ass and worked her mound of venus against his thigh. "You're hot," she whispered. "Christ," he said, invoking God. They went to an empty sideroom. He was just about to get his cock into her, when the night sister came around flashin' her torch. They lay in absolute silence until she'd gone. You'd better go back and drink the tea while I get dressed she said putting on her nickers and stuffing her breasts inside her uniform .

* * *

He needs an injection said the staff nurse, he punched another patient. "I'll see to it," said Wynn. He made the injection really hurt by pushing in the needle and pressing the plunger hard so the fluid bruised the tissues. That'll teach the bastard, he thought.

* * *

MacDuff was a chubby little psychotic who'd regressed to childhood. Wynn was shaving him. "Who's a silly little fucker," asked Wynn. "I am I am," said MacDuff. "What's your name, then?" asked Wynn. "MacDuff. MacDuff. MacDuff," said MacDuff. Wynn kissed MacDuff on his chubby cheek, and said "now fuck off in the ward, and don' tell no mo' lies." "MacDuff. MacDuff. MacDuff," said MacDuff.

Arthur Williams was in the toilet. He shat on the floor. The turd was as big as a swiss roll. Arthur came toward Wynn with clenched fists. Arthur went around with clenched fists trying to hold in his motions as long as possible which accounted for the swiss roll. " 'ad a good shit, 'ave you Arthur?" asked Wynn and shaved him.

That night Wynn moved out of the hospital accommodation and into a flat in Claude road. He lay on the bed and read Dostoyevsky's "Crime and Punishment". Outside the rain came down in buckets.He was fed up with the psychiatric hospital. When you start kissin' patients, he thought, it must be time to get out and get out for good.

* * *

Johnson threw shit out of the hospital window. Johnson was up to buggerin' everybody in sight so the psychiatrists gave him hormone therapy. Johnson developed little breasts, and hips, but he still had his dangler except he could n't get it up to do a bit a buggerin' so he threw shit out of the window instead.

Jim was blind and syphilitic. Johnson and Jim were in the bathroom with Wynn. "Feel his hips, and his little tits," he said to Jim. "Fuckin' 'ell! Marvellous!" said Jim and burst into raucous laughter. “Hey, what’s goin’ on in there,” shouted the staff nurse. “Nuthin’,” said Wynn just bathin’ the nutters.” “Well, get on with it Williams,” warned the staff nurse. “Bollux,” said the syphilitic.

In the Psychosomatic Ward a big dike was chatting up nubile nurses from the General on a two week course.

“Disgusting,” said a nurse from the Rhondda, an ex-miner.

Over the Taff the sun went down, a shimmering gold on the black polluted water with the fire of the cyclops. Far out in the bay ships cut the water to the movement of time on the clock of the coal exchange while the Jewish moneylender in “Crime and Punishment” lay in a pool of blood.

* * *

“The trouble with you,” said a nurse, “is that you don’t finish anything”.

“Mind your own fuckin’ business,” said Wynn.

He did n’t seem to get on with anyone. Everyone got on his wick. It was just like the camp. Everyone knew where they were going except him. The only thing he knew was that he had to keep movin’. He moved into a flat with some musicians. One played a trombone, the other drums, and the third guy the bass. The guy with the trombone worked on the railway, the drummer for the BBC, the bass player was an university drop-out. They were all trying to play blues and worksongs, playing along with records, and having trendy conversations. Wynn bought a trumpet and tried to join in, but they looked at him as if he were daft. It all made him mad.

He tried to make jazz sounds but he had no idea. So in a bit he made out he was a poet and wrote some poems with plenty of words about love and breasts in them, trying to make out he was Dylan Thoms who was very hot at the time. In fact he seemed to lay around the flat with Miles Davies playin' Summertime with Dylan Thomas's "Collected Poems" in paper back in his pocket while reading Dostoyevski.

Eventually, he gave up nursing and went down Guest Keene and Nettlefolds Steel Company. All he did was ask and there he was in a shed with lots of guys in the pool waiting for jobs to come up. One night after work he went to Sophia Gardens with his flatmates, and there she was, his first love, Joy. He went home with her and got his dick into Miles Davies. Only there was not much joy only a lot of grunting and he got the skin off his knees what with thrustin' back and forth on the fuggin' floor and her with a girdle on, too. "Goodnight," he said at the door, and felt her breasts, "I'll see you tomorrow."

"OK," she said,.

He watched the moon sail across the sky among the clouds just like the moon on the camp which was receding now in time except this was n't the camp but the freedom of civvie street. But freedom seemed to scare him more than the camp because he did n't seem to be going anywhere whereas others did. They were going to be nurses and managers and musicians wheras he lived for the moment for mere sensation, for mere experience.

* * *

He was going back to R.A.F.Innsworth when an Arab picked him up. "You ever had a woman," said the guy. Wynn said nothing. "I get you a woman down the dock, get your cock sucked. You ever had your cock sucked by a woman?"

Wynn trembled all over. His uniform chafed him. He felt scared, and excited at the same time.

"I'm gettin' out here," Wynn said.

"No, I take you down dock," insisted the black guy. "Please drop me here," Wynn said, really annoyed now.

Let out he stood on the sidewalk under the bridge and watched the car head down the dock off the Newport Rd and felt relieved.

"Fuckin' wog poof," he said bravely, and put out his thumb at another passing car.

"Get in," said a guy, "I'll take you as far as Gloucester." The guy had a girl friend in Cardiff. He came down to see her every weekend in his car. He did n't drink. He did n't smoke. He saved his money. He had a good job. A real steady bloke, thought Wynn, just like I will be when I get out of this uniform. Time went by. At Gloucester he got out, and caught a bus to the camp, went in the cook house and fried some bacon and egg. You got a lot of perks when you were a dish washer.

* * *

"Hey, did n't you used to box round the fairs?" asked Wynn.

"Yes," said the black nurse.

"You're Winston 'Terrible' Green."

"That's it."

Wynn noticed Winston had very big hands for his size. And no fat at all. Winston also played the piano and sang Ray Charles tunes like "Take these Chains" and others.

"He's lovely," said a poof nurse.

The poofs were very imperious, and haughty. Some of

’em looked at Wynn as though he were dirt. They had their own language, their own attitudes, and were holier than thou. They were feminine and more compassionate as nurses. They were also witty. Wynn envied ‘em. He also felt mad because they seemed to know something he did n’t. He liked ‘em. He hated ‘em. The sun shone ouda their arses as far as the management was concerned and they were protected. They had class. They met in the best hotel in Cardiff and came from all over the valleys like a convention.

One day Winston was caught in a poof nurse’s room. And Wynn knew Winston was an ‘omo, an ‘omo black poof, an asshole shaggin’ son of a bitch, and although he was Winston’s buttie Winston had never tried to shagg him, yet.

And the days went by as before.

Into the hospital came the alcoholics, the tormented homosexuals who attacked their mothers, the psychotics who mumbled to themselves, the paranoids who warned others to stay away, the suicides, and the demented who shit the bed.

One day Wynn was told to go into Cardiff Central Police Station. The patient sat in the darkened cold cell with his knees drawn up to his chin. And Wynn realized these nutters were pathetic, and he felt some compassion for them.

“Come on,” he said, “we’d better go back to the hospital you’ll be safe enough there.”

Outside the station the moon went by through the sky at what seemed a great speed of knots, but it was only the rain clouds and the November wind fuckin’ up his perception.

* * *

"I love you," he said to the girl as he kissed her red lips and explored her mouth with his tongue. She was very tooth pastey. She got hold of his cock in her fist and rubbed it with soap — he had just come home from Guest Keene & Nettlefolds. "You got a beautiful prick," she said. After awhile he got cramp in it.

* * *

Wynn was in Fortune Green Road, West Hampstead. "You gotta get up!" he said to the kid. The kid had a hell of an hangover from boozin' all afternoon. Somehow, they managed to get to the pit orchestra of "Oliver" in the West End. The kid could read anything with his perfect pitch 'an all. And he got a hell of a lot of money for playin' the Oliver gig.

But Wynn was rhythmically stupid and rhythmically daft. Anyhow he pretended he was a poet just like Dylan Thomas. Joy came up to see him, and after he'd fucked her on the bed in Fortune Green Road she began to cry again about her father and mother. "I'm just a suburban girl," she said.

Next day Wynn picked up a young French kid on the tube and fucked her also in Fortune Green Road. "what's that on your wrist?" he asked. She spoke in French, but he knew she'd tried to cut her wrists sometime in the past. Bugger this, he thought, I'll be glad to get to that working man's college.

* * *

The Lleyn Penninsular was utterly beautiful across the bay. Blue, purple, azure the lot, and when the sun went down it was all on fire. The night brought little angels down ladders of light. The camp was a long way away and so were the Communists, and the Russians and the gum-chewing Yanks.

“What’s God got to do with it,” said a student, “God is in the Mind. The Mind has been separated from the body by a process of systematic doubt, that is, doubting the existence of the material world.”

“God is real,” said the Christian, “God is the absolute embodiement of Goodness and Righteousness. He leads us spiritually into the light from the midst of darkness."

“Metaphysical twaddlc.”

“The moon appears to be shining only it is in reality a reflection of sunlight from the other side of the world. This is called Appearance. You live in the world of appearances. God is reality.

“Appearance is our perception of the world and it is in essence true. There is no such thing as the separation of Appearance and Reality.”

“Physical ideas are only Ideas in the mind. If you look at the table from the top it appears a perfect circle that has no legs. Viewed from the side it appears elliptical. So what is the real table.”

“This is the real fuckin’ table," said a student and slammed his fist on the top. The cups and saucers were scattered everywhere.

Fuckin’ nutters, thought Wynn, who understood not a word. So he began posing as a musician with his trumpet except he could n’t count beats, and also he had his poetry to rely on. So all in all he was doin’ pretty well except when the exams came he failed them. And some of the students looked at him with pity in their eyes. They were all so clever except him. He studied the plot of a Shakespearean play. He figured that a character who entered and exited and then entered again had gone so far in between that he'd simply not had the time to get back and enter.

"You have to develop a suspension of disbelief," said a tutor and everyone laughed.

I might be gettin' somewhere, Wynn thought.

In the picture room - the picture room had murals of working people in factories and pits - there was a girl who was always listening to Joan Baez protest songs. Her name was Pristine. She was an Anarchist and believed in free love, and to be free of everything : free of monopoly capitalism, free of Stalinist bureaucracy, free of racism, free of exams, free of envy, jealousy, and of religion. One night Wynn took her to the pictures in Barmouth and kissed her. He always had that feeling of warmth and security when he sat next to a dame in the pictures....

- in Aberdare Rex Cinema after great deliberation he put his arm around this dame he'd picked up in the Aberaman Welfare Dance Hall, she did n't object so after awhile he leaned over to kiss her and accidentally brushed against her bosom. She said : "if you do that again I'll call the manager." He froze. And looked miserably at a lousy black and white film all night: escorted her like a gentlemen to the bus stop in the rain and said goodnight, still in misery . . .

O, Pristine, he thought, you did not call the manager as that bitch did long ago before the camp and the damn gum-chewing Yanks when I was young and innocent and working in Penderyn Limestone Quarry, and my father was alive in the Pandy level workin' his bollox off. No, we are comrades together, studying for a better world in Working Man's

College. But, unfortunately, I understand very little of anything.

He looked up at the little wall lights in the cinema. He loved the little wall lights. They were like flowers in the dark. And there was his love sitting next to him. An anarchist who did nt't give a damn about anything.She was free.

* * *

The exam results came. He'd failed. One guy looked at him with pity. That is, utter pity, and sorrow. He was twenty-eight posing as a poet and trumpet player, and he could n't understand anything in a Working Man's College.

Over the bay the sun went down casting its cosmic spell on the sea in unparalleled beauty, green, orange, and azure. And it was the last time he would see it because his time at college had come to an end. And he was n't going anywhere as usual. So he went to London to Pugh's old landlady in Clapham Old Town and got a job in the civil service as a clerk. Pugh with whom he laid in a cave to the sound of the same sea along time ago. But Pugh had gone and no-one knew where. Nobody cared, either.

* * *

Wynn joined a poet's workshop in Earl's Court, and submitted some poems for discussion. A well known BBC producer was there and other well known poets like an Australian with a flat face like Thomas the Tank Engine. The BBC Producer had a tie of roses and talked with a lisp through his buck teeth. He was an Oxford man. Everbody sucked round him like leeches while others looked toward him for approval.

When Wynn read his poems he got no approval. Nothing happened except polite little criticisms of words and phrases here and there. Well, he could n't have expected more, after all he was a failure just down from a Working Man's College.

* * *

He went to Woking to see a girl he'd met at Bangor University. She was from Merthyr Tydfil, and her dad worked in Hoover's Factory. She told Wynn she got pregnant at Bangor and took a lot of asprin to get rid of it. She was blonde with large full lips and a large nose. Her body had tremendous a lower bulk from her hips to her thighs while her breasts were small. She was very passionate and bit the inside of his lips when she kissed him, pulled his hair and rubbed his genitals like a scrubin' board. . . .

-the scrubin' board was a washboard which was used by American Negroes for rhythm and played with thimbles. Suds ran down his mother's scrubin' board in Rhigos Halt from vigorous action with a clenched hand . . scrubin' boards were common in working class households before the advent of the washin' machine . .

his cock got hot as an iron from Violet's rubbin, and so he shuvved his hand down her panties and rubbed her clitoris, they were rubbin' each other real good when he came prematurely all over his best trousers. "look what you done," he gasped, but she kept on rubbin', her hand full of his soap bubbles. And that was in Clapham Old Town SW4.

"I've changed my mind about marryin' you," he said to Violet, "I got no job and I'm not goin' anywhere."

"You bloody well told me," she said, her nickers were down across her thighs, suspenders undone, her mouth red with smudged lipstick, her pale blonde cheeks flushed, and her straw coloured hair in a mess. "You bloody well promised."

"But I'm not goin' anywhere."

"Who bloody cares. You said you wanted to talk about gettin' married."

"Well, I got carried away. Everytime I thought of you I got an 'ard on, and I thought well I'm twenty nine and I ought to get married and I thought of you and I thought we'd get together and discuss it and here we are but I'm not sure now because I got lots to do, and nowhere to go, that is, yet, and that's not fair on you is it?"

She pulled up her nickers, and fastened her suspender belt, and he grabbed her again seeing her white thighs bulge over the stocking top, and they began to wrestle in the doorway again. "You're a bastard," she said, grabbin' his wet cock. And that's the last time he saw her in his landlady's in Clapham Old Town and felt bledy relieved, but did n't know why after all she was passionate and incapable of real anger.

* * *

He was in Brighton working in a cafe for a Greek. The Greek was a bad tempered bastard who hated Wynn with a great intensity. Wynn was afraid of the Greek. The Greek also had a an Italian guy workin' as a cook. The Italian had no papers and so the Greek protected him and gave him a job. The Italian was OK. He told Wyn that the reason the Greek disliked him was that he, the Greek, was an illiterate bastard who hated everyone who could read and write. But since Wynn was the butt of the Greek's hatred he did n't believe the Wop one bit. He thought the Greek hated him because he, Wynn, was a nobody, a proletarian, without money, without power. That much he'd learned from the Working Man's College. He was a proletarian wanker, and a student at twenty six years of age going nowhere. Except, why the hell did Violet want to marry him. Maybe he had something after all. A good healthy dick.

The Greek's cafe was a pick up joint. One day a bloke with curly hair came in there posing. Everything about him was a pose. The guy had a haughty appearance with an underlying stupidy that fixed him in a kind of vacuous social slot like one of these model blokes in a glossy mag. He had a sports car. A good lookin' dame said : "he stood without his shirt in the rain. What a man!" What's that supposed to mean? "He stood in the rain like a man." Stupid cow. At some other time Wynn picked up a young dame in the cafe and took her to his bed sit in a three story Regency house with a portico in Brunswick square.

The room was in the back with a big glass sky-light on which the rain beat down pitter patter. The girl had a lovely slim body but there was something wrong with her hip joint. She'd had an op and could n't open her legs properly so they could only have sex dogie fashion. She was a really nice kid. Jesus, he thought, a little thing like that could make everything very awkward for her. He never saw her again.

Then there was another dame who was a nurse. And he took her back to the attic room. (He'd changed rooms by now). She kept sayin' "I'm a karate black belt," everytime he tried to steal a kiss. So he gave up on her. Time went by. He sat on the toilet and a knock came on the door, a heavy knock. Insistent. He got up from the toilet without wipin' his ass. Two cops wanted to interview him. There'd been a murder on the London to Brighton train. They wanted to know where he was. "Working as a waiter," he said. So the cops pissed off and he finished wipin' his ass.

When he got lonely he wrote to Merthyr Tydfil, but got no reply. Then he got mad because a Turk pinched the bonus money the Greek had promised him. The Greek was a rat. Wynn told him he'd been stationed in Cyprus to impress him. But it did n't impress the Greek at all who hated him all the more. Anyhow, if the Greeks hated the Turks how the fuck was it the Turk was Greek's best mate? Wynn did n't understand these foreigners one bit, besides they were exploiting him.

One day a friend of Wynn's came from Cornwall and they fucked off to London. On the way the car broke down - the cylinder head had cracked. Wynn abandoned his mate and hitchhiked to London because he was really scared of the Greek. For that he felt ashamed. He should have stayed to help the guy. But that's how it goes, he thought. And the days went by. The sun shone. It rained. It was warm. It was cold. And his memory of events telescoped. He was in London with Robert Jones. Robert Jones had no self-esteem problem. He was goin' places. He was in the Royal Philharmonic Orchestra which was a long way from Hirwaun Bandroom with that stinkin' urine bucket and the rain beatin' on the door. "And who am I?" asked Wynn. But there was no reply.

So he got a job in Madame Tussaud's as an attendant, and they gave him an uniform. Down in the Chamber of Horrors there was an effigy of an attendant, and so Wynn stood next to the effigy and frightened the customers. Great fun.

One day he went into the Baker Street tube station buffet and saw one of the attendants, a Pole, in there. Wynn went over to have a lunch time chat, but the man gathered his sandwiches and went to another table. Wynn was mad. "Fuckin' Polack," he fumed. "There's some funny fucking bastards around," he said to Robert Jones. And they both remembered the Polack in Aberdare Park with twenty six stab wounds and although Fabian of the Yard came down they never did find who did it.

“It must be the war," said Robert Jones, "that fucked 'em up.” And went off to play in the symphony orchestra. In a month or two Wynn went off to the Working Man’s College and read about Pilsudski, but understood not a word. The Polacks were no account fuckers unlike the Russians who were frightening the hell ouda the Yanks and the British ruling classes, that much he knew. About this time he joined the Communist Party.

* * *

It was sometime after the war, and there was a Hostel for Displaced People in Hirwaun. The Bracchi shop there had a one-eyed Italian owner with a cap pulled over his forehead. His name was Lou. Wynn’s father came home from the mine complainin’ about the Wops hangin’ around the counter while he wanted his fags. “They’ve interviewed the lot of ‘em,” said his father, “but found nothing. Fabian will want to know where that Nazi knife is you lost.” Wynn said nothing and went out to play. His father knew everything. And all about the Rhondda Valley. In fact Wynn’s grandmother went to Pennsylvania to work in the pits, but the mine owners were such a bunch of Capitalist swine that she came back with her brood to Glynneath and that was where his mother met his father who drank beer with his mouth open and his teeth showin’. “Drunken swine,” said his mother.

* * *

Wynn tore out the pages of his report from Cefn Coed Grammar School. And his father said: “look he’s ashamed of himself.” And the rain beat on the windowsill. Next week he went to work in Penderyn Limestone Quarry to the deafening noise of crushed stone and dust. "I got him out of the mine," said his father.

And his mother said: "he's a worker now." And rain beat on the windowsill. And the silent radio lay on the small table and fire flickered in the grate, and the clock ticked on the mantelpiece. And the days went by one after another as before.

*　　*　　*

———o0o———

"Am I a witch to be burned at the stake for facial hair
Am I to be condemned for being a woman?
How many in psychiatric hospitals in despair,
Hysterical, and left to rot in the can?"

5

CASTELL BLODAU: 1974

(Castle of Flowers)

"Ged out you chauvinist pig. You coal mining . . . You beer swillin' son of a bitch. You man's man."

Tears ran down from her eyes. Her mouth was twisted in rage.

Her moustache raw after shaving without cream.

"Ged out! Ged out!"

"You wanna see a psychiatrist you do."

"You wanna see one you mean, you malajust.."

"You can ged out."

"No, you ged out!"

"Where to?"

"A bed sit."

"A bed sit? I'm not goin' to any bedsit at my age. I'm a married man now I am."

"Married? It takes two to make a marriage."

"Two?"

"Two people working together to build . . .

"That's what I'm doin' . . ."

"No, you're fuckin' not."

"Hey, stop swearin. My mother don't swear, and I don't expect . . ."

"Rubbish! Whad you know what she does? Are women angels?"

"Well, they're supposed to be."

"You make me sick, Wynn."

"Look! This can go on endlessly. I'm goin' out."

"Out where?"

"To the pub."

"Over my dead body."

She barred his way at the door with her arms outstretched and her legs crossed tightly together like Jesus Christ on the cross. Tears ran down her face, not of mere anger but of frustration and rage, a kind of revolutionary rage.

"Ged ouda the way you stupid bitch, or . ."

"Ow!" she gasped as if he'd actually punched her. "You dare go to the pub," she warned, "and you'll never come back here. Never."

"Don't be so stupid," he pleaded.

"We women are not stupid. We can do anything, and be anything we want to be. We women will be free of the likes of you, you chauvinist pig, you beer swillin..."

"Ged out of the way, you nutter!"

"No! Never."

"You can't stay there forever in that ridiculous posture in that endless stupid rage like some bledy martyr."

"Martyr?"

"Ged out of the bledy way."

"Never!" "Well, you can't stay there all day."

"Can't I? You're not goin' to that pub, and that's final."

"Bully."

"Bully? That's rich comin' from a beer swilling pig like you. I know what you lot are, expecting their wives to sit passively in the house while the men's men jaw in the pub, and come home to eat their cooked dinners like pigs. The miners wives are just skivvies if you ask me.

"No, they're not. They know their place that's all"

"Know their place?"

"Why do you turn every statement into a question?"

"What?"

"Oh, never mind."

There was silence. It was not always like this, he thought. They had companionship in London, well, a little bit of it. What they had was a common feeling of helplessness in being pushed around by everybody. He'd met her in the Poetry Society and was attracted to her wide eyes and her intelligence. After all he was a failure just up from Working Man's College, and she was an university drop-out pushed around by everybody. She lived in a bedsit you could n't swing a cat around in. He lived with a bunch of failures in Twickenham. She fucked like a stoat, and so they went to live in Paddington with a belling stove and a radio. He listened to Howard Winston win the World Featherweight Title on it.

Next, they got a room in Putney with a nutty landlady who she quarrelled with because she burned the stew while out playing tennis in the park. After the quarrel she lay on the floor stiff as a board which became a mannerism among other things like slammin' fuggin doors, and stompin' everywhere like a cart horse. He'd made a mistake for an ill-planned life, and it all went back to his schooldays to his bledy father, and all that anti-school luggage he carried, being led down the mine at fourteen by those capitalists in the Rhondda, the Llewelyn's and the Powell Dyffryns, and all their puritan work ethic bullshit. He'd made a mistake and he'd have to live with it. She was repulsive layin' on the floor stiff as a fuggin' board, shaving that moustache once a bloody week, and with those hairs on her tits. Christ all mighty. Another thing she wanted sex all the damn time, and if he'd did n't give it to her she lay there snivelling in the dark.

Then there were all those demands for affection. "Do you love me?" and "You don't love me do you?" and "My brother committed suicide." and "My father married the district nurse in a week of my mother dyin' of cancer." Holy fuck what a mess! And cryin' about the least thing, on the floor like a fuckin' board. And not likin' any man 'cause all men were pigs: barmen, coal miners, bricklayers, lawyers, school teachers, storemen, taxi-drivers, and lorry drivers. All pigs. What with all the trouble he had with his low wages, and no fuckin' prospects she had to complain about every prick in the town.

It's a lucky thing he did n't get punched to fuck for sayin' "Hey mate, watch what you'r sayin' to my wife!" After all this was a dock town and there were some really fuckin' hard men walking about who thought they were a bunch of Marcianos.

He spent everynight after work doin' his correspondence course in English Literature "A" Level while she, when she was not crying or layin' on the floor stiff as a board, went to the local teacher's training school. One day they went there to play tennis, and out came the Principal, a dame, pissed as a coot. "Don't play tennis there hic hic," she said, "it's hic hic forbidden. Go on bugger awf hic hic."

And time went by as before.

Why did he marry? She was very intelligent and wrote quite passable poetry under his tuition, all personal stuff, how she *felt* all the fuckin' time. Also, he felt he wanted to help her and, of course, she fucked like a stoat. Besides, he could see her parents were well off, livin' in a suburb. After all her dad was a head teacher in a primary school while Wynn's mother was an uneducated domestic servant on Income Support and a miner's pension that did n't amount to much.

"This girl is bloody useless. She can't cook. She don't bloody clean. Oo! Get rid of her." And. "Why did n't you marry somebody like me, boy?" All this was really fuckin' helpful, he thought. While he liked to sit in pubs and feel alcohol get a grip of him and so bask in its warm glow Sybil wanted to be walkin' the mountains, and shaggin' behind stone walls. One time she entered one of the Mellte's pools and swam in it bollock naked with her bean bag tits and her moustache. Some fuckin' freak dame. Then she demanded he fuck her just to keep her from freezin' from that mountain water.

That pool was a long way from Earl's Court, he thought, and that bedsit you could n't swing a cat in. And the Poety Society, and Putney tennis courts, and the crazy landlady. All these Londoners were the same. They filled up every room with lodgers so they pay the godamn rent. Time went by.

She lay on the bed with her legs apart. "Here," she said, "take these." She handed him some plastic calipers of a sort. "Insert them," she said. The calipers opened up her vagina. He could see the vagina was coloured a pinky red and was serrated and at the end an eye looked at him, also pink, and that was the cervix of her womb. She got up from the bed and said: "we've got to learn to examine ourselves. We don't want these male doctors strappin' us to beds and peerin' up us." Fuck all this, he thought, her genitals were absolutely disgustin'. He preferred the mysticism of sensation, besides if he wanted to be a pill pushin' fuckin' quack he could've gone to Ireland and got a phoney licence like everybody else.

Remember that doctor in Glynneath, he thought, a Scotsman by the name of Stuart. Who sat under the window with the light pourin' onto his desk with a Players fag stuck in his mouth, and "Cough! Cough! Splutter! Splutter! What can I do for you?" he used to say. "Cough! Splutter!" A long time dead doctor. Did he open his mother's vagina with a calipers and watch the eye of her womb wink at him? More time passed as before.

"Whad were you doin', then, you bastard with your double morality!"

"Double morality?"

"Chauvinist pig, beer swillin' braggart stompin' around with your dirty cock stuck into any hot bitch you come into contact with. Why should I be any different?"

"Different! You're supposed to be a woman. You're supposed to be modest. Now, I find you've had more cocks than I've had cooked dinners."

"Bastard."

"And look at the idoits you've had. That shyster from Ystrad who thinks he's a one band revolutionary movement. Then there's that burglar, and what's the other one oh that squat little rugby player with the Desperate Dan jaw and a brain the size of a pea.

"He'd knock your fuckin' block off."

"Shad yo' fuggin' mouth!"

And he got up and put his fist through the windows. Smash! Crash! They splintered and cut his knuckles, blood sputtered out of his skin and down his shirt and she squealed like a stuck pig or like that frog his mother grabbed one summer's night and threw out of the house.

“Ged out! Ged out!”

“This is my fuggin house.”

“No it’s not, it belongs to the cobler. The cobler will get you out you fuckin’ maniac.”

“I’m no maniac. It’s you.”

“Me?"

“It’s you drivin’ me crazy.”

“Grow up!”

“You're nuthin’ but a whore, a cheap whore, who flaunts herself round every piece of trousers in the town. What were you doin’ in the room dancin’ with that thief for, holdin’ hands, and belly rubbin’ you stupid fuckin’ bitch . . you've got no shame.”

“Shame! Whad a fuggin’ Victorian idea. Shame? That’s it! What’s good for the goose is good for the gander. Oh it’s alright for you to go fuckin’ that Croat up in the St Cynog Flats is it, but its not good for me to have a lover.”

“SHADDUP! YOU BITCH.”

“Hey, what’s goin’ on in there?” said a voice.

“Whazat?”

“Somebody knockin' on the door.”

He opened the door to a pale face with ginger hair.

“Hey, mate, what's goin’ on? I got a kid tryin’ to sleep downstairs.”

“Oh sorry. I’m so sorry.”

Inside the room they sat and watched each other in stony silence until he got up and washed his hands under the tap, feeling the stinging wounds smart. Tears were running down his face, the beginning of a nervous breakdown. “I’m going down the pub,” he said. She did n’t reply. Outside the moon shone in the sky and the first November frost painted the rooves of the town a pure crystalline white.

It was n't always like this. In the beginning he liked her. She was lost and she told him things about her family and it was all so tragic. She hated her step-mother who came from the back-to-back slums of Derbyshire or so she said, but people lie all the time. It was all so tragic, the mother who died of cancer, the brother who committed suicide, the horrid step-mother. He knew he was onto something there, a great tragic story. And someone who fucked like a stoat with all that body odour and clumps of hair under her arms. And really hot genitals. She told him stories.

Her first love while in the sixth form was an African black who broke her in. And who wanted to marry her, so she took him home. Her parents were appalled. "That put paid to them as liberals," she said. He nodded sagely. Typical bloody liberals. Her father married her step-mother almost a week after his wife had died. Unfeeling bastard, he thought. And she hated her father. No wonder, he thought, the liberal phoney. Another thing was her father was a shit, no doubt about it. He sat around and said nothing, and when it was a meal time he got up and stuffed his face and that was it. He did n't seem to have any thoughts on anything. So why did she hate her father?

She was fuggin' sick that's why only he did n't know it at the time. She was intelligent, that was it, yeah, she'd been put on the Oxford University trail, studyin' extra curricular stuff like Latin, and she'd failed. She was an Oxford University candidate failure set up by a third rate comprehensive school. Fuck, what a mess, and he was a failure from a Working Man's College. Their lives stank of failure.

The dirty flat at the top of the stairs with the rain comin' in, and with a thief livin' downstairs who broke in when they were on holiday and stole a fuckin' valve from the televison set, except he could n't prove it. The whole place stank of failure.

The back bedroom seemed to hang out onto the street, a bit like a livin' in a balloon that was about to blow up any minute. You had to cross the landing to go to bed in view of the downstairs tenants. The whole place stank of failure. The furniture stank of other people and other rooms. All second hand stuff for second hand lives who had in reality just began. Whad a fuggln' mess!

One day he took his mother to see his in-laws. His mother was just a simple uneducated woman who thought in Welsh, who thought in terms of the village. She sat there in absolute silence. The shit father said nothing to her, nor did the back-to-back bledy nurse. His mother sat there with her purse full of miner's union pension ready to go down the pub, but no fucker moved. She leaned over and said to Wynn : "O, I'm bloody bored." And he felt sorry for her 'cause he was bledy bored, too. His mother had been a domestic servant and seemed in awe of this primary head teacher, a fuckin' English shit.

After that she said nothing of the family. Never a thing like "Ooo, he was a lovely man, or such a gentleman." Nuthin'. She said nuthin'. Contempt was in them though. It was there hidden beneath the surface, contempt for the uneducated, contempt for those who never stood up for themselves.

Contempt for the repressed fuckin' stupid Welsh speaking Celts, only these English were n't any different. They were just stupid functionaries of the capitalist system of education who half educated children to be factory skivvies, and learned in the art of obsequiousness to the corrupt ruling classes.

Joe Maisey was from the tenant farmer stock, dull and

stupid in his lassitude, a moral coward. Fuck 'im. Wynn took his proletarian, Welsh mother home. He seethed. And fucked Sybil's hot genitals, and felt disgust for her boney, muscular, thin man's legs and moustache and bean bag tits. But she was intelligent and had attractive eyes, and they talked about poetry and played chess. So it was not always like it was now, they had hope for the future.

"Do you love me?" she asked.

"Yes," he replied.

They went to bed and he kissed her, but her moustache had grown and it was bristley like a man's, and he felt he was kissin' a man, and he wanted to kiss a woman, but she seemed half man. What a mess! Half man with her bony legs, and moustache, and bean bag tits with hairs on her nipples, snivveling in the dark of a damp flat in a room that seemed to hang in space. Whad a mess?

Every night he sat down and did his correspondence course on Shakespeare, and Chaucer and Virginia Wolf, and his precis exercises, until at last he decided to go to the night school and enrol there. The teachers were useless. One guy just read from a Shakespearen play all night without giving any indication he understood the language. The other guy got the examination board wrong so he had to take a quick change in the curriculum. Whad a fuckin' mess! And time went by as before.

Outside the flat the rain came down and worked its way into the chimney and into the front room in a sheet wetness that made you shiver and cough. Next door the landlady screamed at the truck drivers.

"Breakfast you lazy louts, rise and shine."

"Righto! Mrs," they shouted.

The local music shop went into mourning because the

proprietor's brother committed suicide in London. He had made the big time only to end in no time. And the moon came and went, and the ships cut the horizon and the councillors took their bribes and went to jail.

The communist party looked to the Soviet Union and organized the tenant associations – the local taxi driver, a coach builder, and a guy from Newcastle who was appalled at the local apathy set about reforming attitudes with a wife whose tits bulged from a low cut dress even in winter making the apathetic members tremble in their boots. Then, unaccountably, they disappeared back to Newcastle and everyone was relieved.

Every Saturday morning Wynn took the Morning Star to houses three miles apart.

A woman said: "I can't take it anymore because I gotta pay the insurance money instead."

Another said of her husband: "he drinks milk and coughs up blood."

Outside the rain hit the privet hedge with a vengeance. The sun nor moon was seen for several days. Then everything froze over when Spring should 've been there with the sun hinting of a new millenium. One night a fellow student took him home by car. She was blonde and aggressive, she had a complex working as clerk at the university and decided to get a few "A" Levels. She had great fleshy thighs and a skirt riding up over them. He got out of the car with an 'ard on and that night he fucked Sybil's hot genitals with inordinate ardour dreaming of the blonde, and lay on his back in the overhanging bedroom disgusted with himself and his life. Bite the bullet he said to himself.

Come summer he sat his "A" Level and got a D grade and Sybil helped him get to an interview in Manchester. And he got a grant from the town hall.

Time went by as before indifferent to all mortals. Time which is secreted by events, under the moon, under the stars in the movement of molecules that cannot return to their original state as the universe expands into future time. And he watched time in the shadow of his hand creep along under the sycamores in the street, in the shadows of the brawling sparrows, in the eaves, and the evening windows. Across the street in the high room a naked woman combed her hair in the mirror, and he climbed on the roof from the fire escape.

"What are you doin' up there?" asked Sybil, irately.

"Oh, I thought there was a slate loose," he replied.

Many times the woman walked the room opposite naked, and in the street he saw she was beautiful with a broad face and a strong female jaw and when she walked she thrust her hips forward in a swinging movement while she held her back straight so her breasts were also thrust forward. She looked ever so healthy with her white luminous skin.

A desire formed for her as he gazed through the curtains trying to catch a glimpse of her whereas Sybil kept saying: "what are you doin' looking out of the window all the time?" And he could only make excuses about the weather and other such silly things. So time went by, and bite the bullet, he thought to himself. And Sybil lay snivelling in the dark, and whining about her dead brother, his lungs full of carbon monoxide, whining about her horrid step-mother from the back-to-back slums, and whining about her wimpish father and her dead mother.

And: "do you love me,"she asked.

And: "yes," he said, "I do."

And he wanted to love her like he loved Joy so long ago now. He wanted her to have Joy's soft skin and hairless, soft fragrant mouth and Joy's large firm breasts without grotesque hairs protruding from ther nipples. He wanted Joy's arms, and her luscious hips, but not her floppy thighs. Oh, Joy had floppy thighs, and a mean mound of venus. Oh, but no-one is perfect, he thought, but this is killing me O Jesus! Oh, what a mess. O Jesus! And every day she went to the Teacher's Training College and do you still love me she whined? But he did n't love her. In fact everytime he looked at her he felt sick.

And sometimes he watched her coming back from the Teacher's Training College with her bony knees, and her huge disproportionate hips, and slouching bean bag tits and disproportionate head and he felt sorry for her. And one day she said: "I've passed my exams."

"That's wonderful," he said, and kissed her right on her moustache, and felt sick. And time went by as before in the shadow of his hand, under the moon, under the stars.

Awhile back he'd met one of his mates from the Working Man's College, a slightly built fellow with a moustache and soft black eyes that looked at you with an expression of wry amusement and puppy love. He had a friend, a Irish catholic. They were soul mates and studied film. In fact they seemed to sit in the darkness of cinemas most of their time. They also sat with Wynn and Sybil and talked of this and that. All trendy stuff about films, and Cream and cannabis. But Wynn did n't like talk of this cannabis shit since he was a communist and did n't go for all that Hippie crap of opening the vistas of consciousness. He could see Sybil was all for it, though, treating him like some sort of cretin. One day Steve asked if he could stay for awhile. Wynn came back and saw a note on the table, it said:

JUST GONE OUT

love and kisses

Steve XXXX

Love and kisses! What the fuck was that supposed to mean? Who was this guy some sort of poof? A hanger on! What? Who in the name of holy fuck writes love kisses on a fuckin' note like a kid?

Rain beat on the windowsill. Gulls flew around in the air and the ships cut the horizon. Some Indonesian seaman was stabbed to death down the dock, and a family died in a fire.

Wynn looked down on Steve from the landing. "I hope you find another place," he said. Steve looked up at him, but the puppy love in his eyes had gone.

"I got rid of him," he said to Sybil, "there's something wrong with the bloke, all that love and kisses puppy dog shit."

"You don't choose my friends for me," she said that night.

Whad the 'ell does she mean by that? he asked himself while she snivelled in the dark, thinking of her dead brother, and her dead mother as he thought of Joy's soft breasts and her milky mouth and in the corners of the bedroom little shadows formed from the passing cars in the street far below as in a dream of existence. And bite the bullet said a voice.

Wynn sat in the corner composing a poem and thought there's a lot of lonliness around and people will do anything to shed the aura of it. They'd steal your wife. That's one thing they'd certainly do. This town is full of alienated assholes. Marx was right alienated assholes all grasping at straws who owned nothing except themselves who they hired out for a pittance just to pay the fuckin' rent to some Jew landlord who walked around with a carnation in his button hole. Someone screwed you at every turn. His employer down the dock paid him as, little as possible. He came home and the landlord screwed him for as much as he could, then some fucker tried to steal your wife alkin' bullshit about films and dope. Bollux. And he got on the roof to see if the dame across the street was combing her hair with her bare ass showin' but there was nothing only shadows and sunlight on the windowpane.

They were making armatures down the dock for electric motors. Wynn worked in the stores and had to order components in a book. Also he had to file industrial drawings. When he drew his wages on Friday he felt a sense of despair because he knew they would n't last the week after the rent and the groceries were paid, besides the boss was always giving him other duties to do like painting numbers on industrial magnets so he built up a big resentment about the boss, and asked him for a raise.

The boss said no. Wynn's hands were tied. There was no union either. His fuckin' labour value was the amount the boss paid him for his rent and clothes. The rest of his labour the boss stole. Fuck that. But he could do nothing. He controlled nothing. When he went in a shop to buy a can of beans and the capitalist fixed the price of the beans in his tinned bean racket. The bean capitalist stole surplus value from his workers who were in the exact position he was down the goddamn dock. For all he knew the armatures were drivin' the bean manufacturing machines. Only the armatures did n't belong to the workers. The armatures belonged to the boss, that is, until he sold them for money a percentage of which was profit, profit off his and others back only you could n't tell 'em nuthin'. They only laughed and said: "he's a fuckin' red." There's no fuckin' future in this, he thought. And he went home and watched Alf Garnett.

Every Saturday morning he took the Morning Star over the hill and watched the rugby match on Saturday afternoon, or maybe the football. It was a kind of happiness, a kind of duty to yourself and to your wife, the kind of life hundreds of thousands were living without property, without future.

And All Property is Theft, he thought, echoing Proudhon, and he thought of Pristine in the Picture Room listening to Joan Baez who promised to end all iniquity with a song. He thought of Pristine's raven black wop hair, and her soft mouth. Oh, she was a tragic little bitch. Look what a mess Alex Comfort and his Free Love had got her into! Fuckin' tragic! All that free this and free that had got her in a hell of a mess. Serves the cow right all she really wanted was bourgeois success.

All she wanted was a degree in the end. And then he felt ashamed of calling her a bitch because that's one thing she was n't. She was a mixed up fool, used by a bunch of pricks for a quick jump, and in the final analysis they were the ones that skipped town in a crisis. Anarchists were pure egoists. Whad were they issuin' party cards for? Jesus Christ there was more political discipline in a fuggin' orgie.

Sybil was cryin' again, tears streamin' down her face and into her whiskers, (she'd not shaved for a week,) cryin' and sobbin'.

"I want, a baby," she gasped, quivering in his comforting arms.

All that shaggin' and gruntin' and snivelling in that room overhanging the street like a bad dream about to burst had come to nothing so out came the thermometers, and the ovulation charts. And he had to have a sperm count after jerking off in an old fish paste jar. Well, his sperm count was OK what was he a man or a mouse? In awhile, anyhow, she conceived. She became a pot bellied bitch gripin' about her weak father and her cancer-dead mother, and her gassed brother, gripin' about men shouting from building sites masculine obscenities as she walked the street with her large head and bony boys knees and disproportionately big ass. Whad a mess! He'd made a mistake and he'd have to live with it. Bite the bullet. Lots of people lived like this, he thought, without being attracted to their wives.

They lived as best they could. They compromised. That's the only thing they could do. Compromise. They lived from day to day in their misery. They did their duty as husbands as best they could, maybe had a little affair on the side. Jerk off over some dame in the office. Look down a bird's dress as she bent over, or up her skirt. Fug, whad a mess! Whad a fuggin' mess! And so the days went by.

Eventually, she lay in the bedroom overlooking the street and told him she was breaking water. It was twelve o'clock at night. Whad a time! Whad a fuggin' mess! He walked to three telephone booths. They were all vandalised. He went to the cop shop, and they gave him a load of lip in among shouts from the cells until eventually they decided to make a a call for him. And so he went back to the bedroom and the ambulance came, and sat glumly in the delivery room.

"Push! Push!" said the nurse, but nothing came.

He could see the crickled head, but the baby would n't pop out.

"Push! Push!" Nothing came. The nurse got a pair of calipers. "Unless you push I gotta use these," she continued.

Sybil pushed,and pushed with perspiration wending its way through her moustache while the hairs on her chin quivered and her horrible vulva opened and out came the kid as dry as dish. The nurse wrapped it up and put it on the scales. It was a girl,and Wynn was a dad. And he went home on the bus and slept.

When he woke up things had not changed. He was still a dad. So tried to clean up the flat for Sybil's home coming. He brushed the carpet. He polished the linoleum. He lit the fire, and dusted the second hand furniture. He picked up a heavy chair and something went crick in his back that dropped him to his knees. He got up and got on the bus but the pain got worse. In while he got to the hospital and gave her some flowers and went away again. She would be out the next day said a nurse. He stood at the bus stop and the pain dropped him to his knees for the second time. A car came along and a guy asked him if he was OK. Wyn said he's got a pain in the back. The hospital discharged him with a spray. He crawled along the corridor and a back specialist happened along.

"Get that bloke in traction," he said.

For the next ten days Wynn lay in traction while Sybil stayed with a friend. Whad a fuggin' mess, he thought, twisting and turning in the traction. And time went by as before in an agony of existence.

"You're a silly little bugger. Shitin' in yo' nappy. Kiss kiss kiss kiss you little dumplin'. Hoochey! Coochey!" he said.

"She's teethin'.'"

"Oh, yeah."

"She's got a nappy rash."

"Oh, yeah! Gotta change her more often, put some more cream on."

And Sybil and Wynn became a mother and a father doing

what mothers and fathers do, gazing at the off-spring with wonder and amazement at nature's magic and its ultimate indifference.

And so the days went by one after another, and the moon traversed the sky. And the ships cut holes in the horizon. And the communist party went on much as before influencing the policy of the labour party, and infiltrating the unions while the capitalists fought a rearguard action, piling lie on lie and confusing reality. And anti-communism that killed Allen Ginsberg's mother Naomi was as rampant as ever. Kill the Commies shouted the American Rednecks while the Russian Soviets entered the arms race and peered over the Berlin Wall at an hostile capitalist world, living with the ghost of Stalin.

Down the wall the water poured sending a shiver through Wynn's lungs, and Sybil wrapped herself in woollens, and the fire crackled in the grate, and the girl across the street combed her hair in the mirror, showing her fleshy hips and buttocks.

* * *

It was a good farm in undulating hills, it even had the services of one farm labourer. Lazy bitch with her bean bag hairy nippled tits did nothing while her Aunt cooked her ass off and laid stews on the table. Wynn was out of his depth economically speaking. He was a proletarian like the land labourer while they were owner occupiers. The farm was good. Wynn just sat around and ate while Sybil sat and ate, too, and lolled in front of the log fire. Happy days. Happy days, that is, until the sick fuggin' Somerset farmer started makin' snide remarks about the unemployed proletariat. This fat lazy subsidized Tory pig who got a wage off the government for raising stock even if he could not sell it was full of self righteous scorn.

Fuckin' Kulak, thought Wynn. They, the familly, sat around the table and stuffed their gullets with beef, Yorkshire puddin' and roast potatoes while the fuckin' proletariat slaved for wages in factories full of fumes and the stink of oil and dust, and lived on beans and fish fingers. Fuck that shit for a start. He imagined kicking the fuckin' farmer in the bollux. They were all fuckin' stupid anyhow. Semi-literate shyters stinkin' of dung milk, and fishy cow-vagina. Another thing he could see Sybil was part of this.

She was of a different class. A lower middle farmin' dispossesed economically ignorant one step up from a peasant ugly in every possible sense milk maid bitch. They were young marrieds with a baby girl Hoochey! Coochey! Kiss! Kiss! And time went by as before changing things in a series of events in which time was secreted, in which the future arose from the present, rose inexorably like the tides of the sea.

Wynn went to a rent tribual and got the chimney fixed so the damp did n't come in so much. The Jewish landlord stood in the doorway and inspected the place with his carnation. A minor victory in the battle against property which is theft.

And then he and Sybil went to Rochdale to a flat with under-floor heating and a view of the John Bright cricket ground. They took their second hand furniture stinkin' of the sweat and breath of old tenants. The flat was warm and dry. They were movin' on, improving themselves, beginning to go places.

Wynn had a pamphlet of poems out.He was a star among students and postgraduates. The world was his oyster.

In every can of beans there is sugar as preservative, he thought, and sugar could only be manufactured in a certain climates, originally in the Caribbean using slaves as commodities, bought and sold in the market place. He fuckin' knew what it meant to be a commodity, selling his labour power for a pittance. His father knew. His father, forced off the land, worked in a filthy mine, and sold his soul to the coal owner . . . . fuck, this can of beans had the history of commodity production built into it as an object. Tin. Was it tin? I bet it's a mixture of elements smelted down, and in every phase the capitalist extracted surplus labour, realized in surplus value as money.

A tin of fuckin' beans said it all. A history of exploitation, and of science in a tin of beans no-one thought twice about. And that was the trouble no-one thought about anything 'cause no-one was meant to because if they knew, and acted out of moral rage they'd all join the communist party. A working man who did n't join the communist party was a sucker, a victim of lies, a victim of the illusion of freedom. The only people who were free were the bourgeoise, but even they were locked in the system like prisoners, going bust all the fuckin' time. And startin' wars.

"I'm going to a woman's meeting tonight," said Sybil, breaking his reverie.

The little girl was about two and walking around under the table exploring this and that and bumped her little head, and bawled out like a banshee. He went over and picked her up.

"Alright," he said. "There, there you dimbo. Hoochey! Coochey! Daddy's little baby."

And time went by in a kind of bliss.

Sybil sat in the bath with cream on her upper lip, and a dab on her chin. Her knobbly knees were raised as though she were rowing a boat. Her bean bag tits were flat against her chest like pig's ears, pink and hot from the water.

"Wash my back," she said.

He washed her back. Her back was hard and muscular with the ribs protruding, and he found two more long hairs on her bony shoulder blades. O God why was n't there a clear demarcation of her sex and why did this make him suffer so? Surely other men had wives with hairs on their tits, and bony knees with large heads and disproportionate arses, but it did n't seem to bother them. Actually the most masculine women were in the working classes, jaws like Rocky Marciano, and legs like Joe Louis: busted noses, varicose veins, hair like horses, coarse and dry. Christ what torment! Sybil stood up. Her buttocks seemed to drop like potato bags.

"I gotta go," he said, disgusted.

"No," she said, "dry me."

Out of her armpits a waft of body odour came.He felt he wanted to retch. Christ, she simply did n't know did she, she simply did n't know how he felt about her body. Disgusting. But there was something about her. It must be her intelligence, he thought, but she had no grace whatsoever Thump! Clump! everywhere. Thump! Clump! And another thing was she was superficial. She glossed surfaces. She never looked for reasons.

Therefore, she was not wise. She had not inherited the wisdom of her sex. She had no self-knowledge. How could she? She was so full of hatred for everything. Another thing there always seemed to be women's evenings nowadays, and women's refuges, and campaigns for toilets, and low wages well, that was progressive enough – but there were other things like women could n't go out alone in the evenings, or travel alone with out being harassed. And only women knew each others bodies. He thought then she was a fuckin' dike. He was married to a goddamn dike, and his daughter would grow up to be a dike. Holy Jesus, it was unthinkable.

"Hurry up," she said "i'm gettin' cold."

And clump! thump! he moved into the front room.

Another thing, she had a really funny shaped head. It was long and thin, and raised at the centre like a medieval war helmet. It made him sick to touch it. What have I done? he asked himself. What Have I done? And bite the bullet.

Down in the Polytechnic there were hundreds of girls all from the comprehensive schools of the north of England. There was something wholesome about them. Young, nubile, at ease with themselves. No fuckin' suicidal brothers, no fuckin' step-mothers. They were all from back to backs anyhow. No dead fuckin' mothers. No hairs on their tits. No heads like medieval warriors. No bony fuckin' knees. Nuthin'. Livin' for the moment in their salad days. He was their poet. But he could n't write. So he drank instead and wept, and masturbated. Wham! Wham! Went the semen. Wham! A glans penis like the head of a gaboon viper, a fuckin' stem like a baby's arm, a pair of massive bollux. Ged a hold of it all! He wondered whether any of these young-sters had fucked a horse like Aneurin did. He wondered whether they could hit a tin roof four feet above their heads like those Welsh fuckers did in Aneurin's shed with the flickerin' candle and the rain beating down and Aneurin's mother shoutin': "Whad are 'ew doin' in there our Aneurin?"

And time went by in its mystical way and with it the tragic human perception which resulted in death which the young in no way worry about. All they cared about was watching each others asses, and tits and Penis Lavender's crutch which was all the rage among the nubile girls of the northern towns.

And Sybil became famous and appeared on TV 'cause she'd discovered some Filipinos working in a sweat shop for next to nothing, exploited by some petite bourgeois northern asshole calling himself a businessman, and what was a businessman but a crook, a thief, a parasite. Why? Because he stole surplus value in the form of money profit from the labour embodied in a thing which was sold on the market as a commodity.

A businessman was a very respectable man, a pillar of society, a man who went to church and worshipped God in medieval replicas of a sadistic fetish – kneeling to a figure on across with a crown of thorns and nails through his hands and feet, portrayed in graphic detail down to the trickle of blood between his toes.

A business man, a demi-god in an inhumane system where every man was himself a commodity bought and sold like a slave in the market place. The word businessman was loaded with emotive meaning and with contradictions that ran through it like undercurrents of a dangerous river.

Businessman with their briefcases, and pinstripe suits. Important men creating wealth. A load of bollux. They created wealth OK for themselves while pushin' others into poverty and wage-slavery.

One day they went to visit her father who had retired in the Cotswolds, an idyllic English backwater. Wynn played football with Sybil's step-brothers one of whom looked uncannilty like Hitler, the other like the 'orrible step-mother from the back-to-backs. Wynn got sick with a temperature of hundred and three, and lay groaning in bed like a big baby. His throat was swollen, everytime he swallowed he swallowed razor blades. Nevertheless, he had to go. His time was up.

Noticing he could n't go by train they bundled him in a car. He lay in a blanket shivering, then he wanted to vomit, but they would n't stop until they got to a car park, backing into the car back he vomited out of the opened door, his head scraping the tarmac Ugh! Woosh! Arrgh! Green bile all over the car floor. In the mirror he saw the back-to-back horror grimace in disgust. Wynn then fell asleep until he was helped staggering into bed two hundred miles away.

After this episode Sybil never again spoke to her father. She was just waiting for some excuse because something had happened in the past, some sort of betrayal Wynn was not quite sure of. It was nuthin' to do with how badly they treated her beloved Wynn who'd picked her up from the gutter.

One day they decided to return to Castell Blodau which was far more a romantic seaport town than Rochdale with its back to backs and redundant mills.

Sybil was now a fully formed feminist. And the root of her feminism was not political but psychological. She was a lower-middle class nutter. She could n't reconcile herself to her gender. It was no fuggin' wonder since she was half man, hairs on her bean-bag tits, a moustache, very bristley, hairs on her chin, (he found some mo' on her thighs, five in fact, with one overlapping the others like counting to five in match sticks,) and BONY KNEES. Oh, God what a mess! No, she could n't reconcile herself with her gender. She hated men in particular, and in general. She hated building site workers. She hated male doctors.

She hated her father. She hated red-faced pig farmers, coal miners, rugby players, publicans and every pot bellied shyster who had to work for a living. She hated herself because she was just plain UGLY in all aspects. She had no physical grace either. She walked like a crab with lead claws, clump! clump! clump! Her mind was harsh, political, argumentative, tense, and malicious — a cloven-hoofed bitch.

"Ged out! Ged out!"

He had just helped her shave underneath her mephitic arms. And put talcum powder on her tits, then the argument just erupted.

"Ged out! Ged out!"

"You ged out."

"No, you."

"Chauvinist pig. Drunken oaf!"

"You're fuggin' nuts. Your whole family's nuts. No wonder your fuggin' brother put his head in the gas oven.."

"Under the car exhaust.." "What fuck difference does it make?" "GED OUT! GED OUT!"

"Your father, (whad an assole!), married that back-to-back harridan when your cancer-dead mother was still fuckin' warm..."

"GED OUT! GED OUT!"

"Dead mother! Dead brother! Hated step-mother! Weak fuggin' father! All this tragedy is an excuse for jumpin' into bed with every Tom, Dick and Harry, humpin' and snortin' in that bed while my daughter slept only two feet away. YOU FUCKIN' WHORE!"

"Ged out! Ged out! You pig. You're nuthin'. A fuckin' nobody: no account bastard. They're all twice whad you are? Pig!"

"Go fuggin' committ suicide!"

It was then he tried to slug her, but missed, and she

started to flap her hands at him in a pathetic attempt at fighting.He tried to punch her again, but his timing was off until a left jab caught her in the mouth. Splat! And the blood discoloured her lips. And as he backed off she grabbed a knife from the the table and came at him, so he disarmed her. Later they sat in armchairs shocked and exhausted. Later still they made love in the bedroom, adrenalin still in their blood. He was shaftin' her hot genitals with his chopper, bang! bang! And new elements had entered their relationship.

Sexual jealousy. Thwarted filial love. Defiance of what is natural, O King Lear! O Othello! O Leontes!

"We should n't have sold the furniture in Rochdale."

"The baby is sleepin' in the back. Anyone can walk in off the street and take her."

"The landlord has not boarded off the the stairs."

"We'll go to a rent tribunal."

They went to a rent tribunal. They got a notice to quit. They moved to a house a long way out. She came home one day after a woman's conference, her feet were bleeding from dancin' with women. Dancing for the shear joy of it without some man pressing his prick into her and wantin' to go outside and wrestle in some alley forcing her legs open.

"We'd better separate," she said.

"OK."

She went to get a flat — every lower-middle, petty bourgeois fly-by-night had a sordid flat to rent with second hand furniture stinkin' of old sweat and fag fumes.

After seeing it she came back weeping with the kid. He . could n't understand. After all the STRONG WOMAN ideas she had been propagating she still looked to him for help.

He went back to Manchester. Whad a fuggin mess! Whad a jam! And you gotta bite the bullet, he said to himself. You made a mistake and you got to live with it every hour, day and night like thousands of others that go to football matches every Saturday in the utter misery of their miserable lives.

"See this tin of beans," he said "if a capitalist enterprise uses more technology to produce more cans of beans then the price of the beans will drop which will in turn reduce the rate of profit and a reduction in the rate of profit means less investment which means a decline in the rate of economic growth so bankruptcies and unemployment will follow.

And all the lights of Manchester went out due to the power worker's strike. And Wynn felt a glow of pride for the militancy of the working class in its fight against capital.

She was beautiful with long blonde hair and translucent soft skin, and when he kissed her her mouth was moist and warm, and she opened her mouth and ran her tongue along his. Holy Jesus! Beautiful. They were in his car in Bowden Vale, and he ran his hand under her sweater. Her skin was smooth like alabaster and her tits were firm and large. No bean bags these. This girl could really smooch. She was a great masturbator. His semen hit the roof of the car.

"Christ," she said, "that's really good, my boy friend can't do that. You're so masculine. My boy friend's a bit effeminate "

Why the 'ell is she tellin' me that, he thought, and dropped her off at her bedsit in a posh middle class area.

"You can't come in," she said.

AND HE FELL IN LOVE WITH HER

O straw coloured hair! O soft skin with fragrance of

oses! O strawberry red sweet mouth! O Breasts of marble! O Hips of Marble! O Thighs of Marble! O Perfect Form! O Perfect Temperament! O Longing! O Desire! O Innocence! And he became Love Sick. Could n't sleep. Could n't eat. Could n't think. O how he needed her: was filled with guilt and anxiety. And when he was with her the pain would go away and he would be at ease in her presence, but she resisted him, and floated away like an Angel and she became Love Sick, pining for him. O Ecstasy! O Heavenly Bliss!

But she was always in a group of people who were controlling her, holding her back from him.And she would break from them and come to him. And one night she came to him in a taxi and they lay on the bed naked, but when he tried to make love to her she turned away. O Foolishness! She was so young and innocent. And his life was too complicated for her.

"Why are you crying?" she said.

"I am carrying the world on my shoulders like Atlas," he said. "I am Prometheus bound to the rock with vultures at my liver because I invented fire.."

"You're nuts . ."

"It's you have driven me nuts," and then he was sorry he said it because he did n't want to burden her with his pain since she was in her innocence and at the beginning of her life, and he felt he was despoiling her.

O Ecstasy! O Bliss! O Love! O Eros! O Aphrodite!

He met her in the coffee bar and showed her some poems. She was a little fat so she wore craft shop clothes and craft shop beads. She took his poems and folded them and put them down her cleavage. Whad the fug is this all about? he thought. Who could understand young dames? And all the time from the corner of his eye he was conscious of the blonde, and conscious of himself, of every action and gesture as though he were an actor on a stage. But he was ridden with guilt about Sybil and torn about his duty toward his daughter.

Whad a mess! Now he and the girl got on a bus and went back to her flat, a sordid, damp bedsitter in a run down former middle class area of Manchester. They lay down on a series of huge velvet pillows she had arranged and kissed then she took off her dress and went into a kind of worshipping posture by raising her arms and breasts up to the moonlight coming in through the window set high in the wall.

In the bed her hot genitals fixed on his were the hottest he'd ever experienced. She was bundle of amorphous flesh smouldering in the heat of the bed like a burnt out fire, hot and musky. He fell asleep between her thighs, his head pillowed on her belly. In the morning he got up and went to the toilet at the end of the landing. Her menstrual blood covered his belly and down along his thighs to his knee caps. He washed himself and went back to her.

WHY ARE YOU CRYING?

"I got to go to a lecture," he said, and went out into the cold damp Manchester morning. At midday he peered into the lecture room to see the blonde. Her name was Ruth and as he talked with her he felt small and insignificant because his feeling for her had overwhelmed him. He was dependent on her charm and good will as child depends on a mother. He was in love he knew. And it was bledy agony.

"This tin of beans is probably made of sheet steel with a

tin coating – tin dioxide SnO derived from the mineral cassiterite found in the Malay Penninsular. Tin is a tetragonal crystaline system, idealized, that is. In this tin of beans there is embodied whole systems of scientific methods – physics, chemistry and all its subdivisions.This tin which has come to mean container is a commodity. In this commodity is embodied labour power exploited at every level for massive profits in every process from raw material to finished product & sold for money.

This product has not at any time belonged to the wage-labourer, it is the property of the capitalist, that is, until I bought it for MONEY. And this Money goes to the Capitalist, but now this tin of beans is mine. And I am using it as teaching device . ."

"BOLLUX"

"Ged stuffed you feminist cow!"

"GED OUT! GED OUT!"

"Where to this is my home?!"

"Daddy! Daddy!"

"She's got her hand in the door jamb!"

"Arrr! Wharr! Boo! Hoo!"

"Ged her hand out!"

The more he moved the door the louder the kid screamed until he did n't know which way to move the door, open or shut.

"You'll break her fingers!"

"Shaddup you stupid cow, and let me think."

"Arrr! Wharr! Boo! Hoo!"

He opened the door and got her hand out.

"Daddy! Daddy!"

There don't cry.

"And don' you cry, either."

Sybil was full of disgust and loathing.

"I've found a flat," she said.

He went back to Manchester to finish his degree. He was still Love Sick. He could n't take it anymore. He wept and wailed, and went to the phone and got hold of his tutor, a gingered haired, pale, quiet, rat of a person who more resembled a reptile than a human being, cold blooded and unfeeling. He was a poet who wrote in little images, cold and prosaic. He was filled with the metal of ambition, and hated Wynn with a cool consistency always marking down his essays and trying to chastise him about fuggin' deadlines. He referred Wynn to another tutor, a Welsh fellow, who came and took him home to the cotton villages east of Manchester.

The tutor was pissed. In the house he started making faces behind his horsey wife's back like a child in a playground. His wife was real big, about five ten. In the morning they all had breakfast. The tutor pissed off into Manchester.The wife took Wynn into the glasshouse and showed him the horses in the garden. She was still in her nightgown. As she stood there pointing to the horses, he could feel the desire emanating from her. He looked down at the slope of her buttocks. He got an unbearable hard-on, but he was too scared to make a move.

"It's very bad at home," said the tutor, "my little girl wets the bed, and has got to go to a psychologist. You think you got troubles."

Fuckin' Jesus Jones, thought Wynn, I gotta ged out o' this. Whad a fuggin' mess! And time went by as before over the roof tops of Manchester, over the Pennines, over Halifax where Reginald Christie fiddled the Post Office and made a run for Ladbroke Grove and murdered all those poor whores so he could fuck 'em dead as dodos : over the cotton warehouses and workers slaving in the ragtrade creating surplus value for capitalists, over the lovers and the students in their cramped little bedsits. Lord have mercy on them! thought Wynn. And Lord have mercy on me, and on George Best!

He set a rigorous timetable for his degree studying up to twelve hours a day, piling through books and lecture notes and essays, cross referencing, and memorizing from little postcards. And he realized how much he did not know and began to panic – weep and masturbate. One day he went to the postgraduate club and met a girl. He'd figured by now that every fuckin' dude in town followed a doll like a bunch of dogs after a bitch, but nobody hung with a wall flower.

That was the trouble with Ruth she had all the dogs after her 'cause she was a real good lookin' lovely soft hearted northern bitch who was Love Sick for him but heckled into order by others lookin' after her welfare. And because they could n't consummate their love they fell into a courtly routine of ideal longing. Bollux. She was gone forever across the Pennines into Sheffield with her effeminate boyfriend to breed and to die like every other fucker taking with her her amourous youthful adventures. O Sybil. Yeah, he'd figured out that the wall flower fattie the overweight were not prized in an age of thinness and there lay his salvation.

He saw her dancing through the crowds. She had pinned back hair and a large jaw with enormous breasts tight under her sweater. When he danced with her she made no effort to go and sit down so they smooched the evening away. He took her home to a middle class suburb, and sat in the sitting room with her. She told him her father was a head teacher, and her mother had died and so he had married the secretary. In fact her father came in with the secretary and went straight up the stairs. The house was real big. In a while after he'd kissed her she took her blouse off and her brassier and let him fondle her breasts.They were great breasts. Heavy, languid like fruit. No bean bags these. No hairs on her nipples. She put her sweater back on and he fondled them over her sweater which was very erotic. Why the fuggin' hell did these kinds of dames go round with brassieres on? Fuggin' capitalism! Fuggin' con-sumerism! She was a natural Zulu. Full of that firm fatty tissue around her ass, around her thighs, around her hips. No fuggin' whiff from her armpits but an aroma of female hormones, sweet and delectable.

Next he met her in a pub. She drank pints of beer and smoked like a fuggin' collier. She reminded Wynn of his father, beer and cigarette smoke. Wynn was very affectionate when he was a kid and often climbed on his father and kissed him. And it was the same smell. Sweet and sickly pub fumes. Wynn pressed her against the wall and took out her breasts while she finished her fag, and shoved his hand down her skirt and opened her vulva and stroked her clitoris. She got hold of his cock and pulled it out just like Violet so long ago but she did n't have Violet's passion. This gal was a back alley lover who'd felt the alley wet wind on her ass while dyin' for a piss after a gutz full o' beer.

She said: "you can do anything but you can't make love to me because they all want to do that especially with two of us."

Fuggin' 'ell, whad did she mean by that? Whad do they all want? Anyhow, he kissed her thighs, her buttocks, her belly, her breasts. O She was a Great Masturbator and He was a Great Masturbator! O they explored each other! O they were Man and

Woman, curious as cats! O his Cock was raw! O her Cunt was raw! It was Little! It was Virgin! It was Elastic! It was the Beginning! It was the End! It was like Joy's so long ago! O First Love! O Betrayal!

WHY ARE YOU CRYING?

"See this can of beans. It embodies labour power. And labour power is only partly paid for by the capitalist class. This commodity is expropriated and sold on the market for a price, but the price of labour embodied in this commodity is paid as wages, that is, necessary labour. The difference between the price paid for labour power, and the price it is sold at is known as profit. PROFIT IS EXPROPRIATED . ."

The rain beat on the window, pitter-patter. The slates on the houses of Manchester shone in the rain. A pigeon sat on the eaves and shivered. Someone coughed in a further room. The light faded and darkness came down and time went by as before in which events were enacted and which gave the human perception of time an element of pathos.

"You're a very sensitive person," she said sitting naked on his lap.

He ran his hand along her thigh, and along her hips and on to her breasts. They sat there like a sculpture.

"See you Thurdsay," he said.

But Thursday was his last exam, and he got in his car and went home to Sybil to try and put the Humpty Dumpty together again, home to the seaport town of Dylan Thoms, and his sea captains, weeping into the rain that beat on the wind-screen through the countryside as he sped through Cheshire and Shropshire, down the A 49 and into Breconshire and the Castell valley where Madame Pattie spent her last days in the Empty Theatre of Life, O Lord.

He and Sybil got together again in a three roomed flat by the sea, and he did a teacher's training course. But too much had happened, too much freedom had intervened, too many erotic encounters, too many irreconcilable ideas. And the rain came down as before. Pitter Patter.

Wayne Holmes, a romantic revolutionary seaman, had slept with her. Wayne Holmes had broken into their house in Dunvant to collect his Giro. Wayne Holmes had betrayed his friendship. Wayne Holmes had fucked Sybil in the little room with his daughter. She'd had more cocks than he'd had cooked dinners. She was a sexually avaricious cow. She'd betrayed him. Down came the rain. Pitter Patter.

WHACK! WHACK! WHACK!!

He hit her round the head until her head was spinning and she saw stars.

"That's the first time I've ever seen stars," she said.

And the women's refuge was beckoning. She was a heroine. She was at the vanguard of the struggle against the chauvinist pigs while he had to protect this girl from herself. She'd tried to be strong, a strong sister, but had not come up to par. She needed protection. His daughter needed protection.

He was, after all, a husband with all the responsibility that entailed. He was a bully and a brute. An inadequate. An alcoholic. He was a man. But what was Sybil? She was only twenty four. She remembered her school days, that African, the racist father, the dead brother, the dead mother. The playground of the comprehensive, the sixth form. The teachers. And this was marriage! And this was adult life! Whack! Whack! She wept. He turned away. He wept. The rain came down. Pitter. Patter.

Wythenshaw had six kids and a wife. When Wyn went

to Wythenshaw's flat on the St Cynog Estate he was greeted by the whiff of urine and faeces. The kids pissed the bed. Pissed on the floor and pissed over each other. They also shit their nappies and shit on the floor. Wythensahw was a satirical writer who had a hundred rejection slips from Punch Magazine and had formed a relationship with the Editor because of this.

His wife was an anarchist and believed in free love so Wythenshaw did n't know if all his kids were his or not. All he knew was that he had to look after the lot o' em.

Wythenshaw said: "you two will never get on."

Wynn said: "whad about you and Nestor?"

Wythenshaw said: "we'll never get on either."

Wynn said: "whad will we do?"

Wythenshaw said: "nuthin' "

And down came the rain. Pitter Patter.

Sybil and Wynn separated because the landlord got a court order from a fuggin' judge and they were homeless. They got another flat owned by a cobbler. And Wynn smashed the windows, and Sybil put his belongings — two suitcases on the landing — and Wynn got a bedsit.

Wythenshaw said: "how can you be jealous of someone who makes you sick?" Wynn said: "I don't know." Wythenshaw said: "she's not a piece of property." Wynn said: "I've heard that before somewhere?"

He went back to Wythenshaw's. The kids pissed over Wythenshaw, and shit on the floor. His wife came in and they pissed over her. She went into the kitchen but there was no food in there, and Wythenshaw asked Wyn for some money to buy some food and Wynn gave him some. Wythenshaw then went out to get some milk and some tea and Nestor made a pass at

Wynn. Nestor had a nice soft mouth and no moustache, but she had bean bag tits after all those kids.

"I can't do it," he said, "because of Mike."

She said nothing. She was impassive. And he wondered what made a nice girl act like that. Women are very complex, he thought.

And down came the rain. Pitter Patter.

The kids in the comprehensive school loved student teachers. When Wynn went into the classroom they asked him where he was from and if he played rugby for Wales. He told 'em to shaddup and do as they were told. That was a big mistake. After that instead of talking to him they started to talk to each other. Loud. Wynn told 'em to shaddup.

"SHADDUP! SHADDUP! SHADDUP!"

And they talked louder and louder. Some girls looked out of the window at the rain. Some boys did homework from another lesson. Some drummed on the desk tops.

Wynn abandoned his lesson plan and kicked over a desk with a karate snap kick. This did not impress the kids who talked and giggled, and giggled and talked. Down came the rain. In came the deputy head and asked why there was a desk on the floor. One kid said the teacher kicked it over. Out went the deputy head and wrote a report.

Wynn went home in his car stopped at an off licence and bought a bottle of whiskey, and cried his eyes out. Down came the rain. Next day he met Judith. Judith Evans was from Pontypridd. She was a real boozer and an expert on the Mabinogion. She had freckles and was tall with a big bust and a big ass. He sat boozin' with her.

WHY ARE YOU CRYING? asked Judith.

"My father's dead and I'm all alone in the world. My mother does n't understand me, and neither does my wife."

"You're so sensitive," she said.

All the students were writing essays. They had so many essays to write that they copied passages from books, and deleted the adjectives. Then they swopped essays, and added some adjectives of their own. They deliberately misspelt things like they were supposed to do according to Kingsley Amis, and other right wing ogres who thought the proletariat should n't have an education. This course was one of the worst. There was too much work. There were too many students. You could n't get books. The tutors were arrogant, and superior, or just stupid. They were school teachers who made good. They were liars.

They were cunning, and devious. They told the truth only if it suited them, and the truth rarely suited them. They were concerned only with discipline because without discipline you could not teach, and so others could not learn. They knew a lot you did n't know, and used it against you. They knew who the dissidents were. They liked to see fear, and smell it as it emanated from people. They disliked the outspoken.

They were the guardians of the system that taught bourgeois economics that perpetuated class, and jealously guarded their social status based on knowledge and the withholding of knowledge that made them powerful. They were petty, and vindictive and without principle if challenged in any way. The government depended on them in a crisis, and the crisis was that the system was threatened by the presence of the Soviet Union and its doctrines of working class freedom.

And down came the rain. Pitter Patter.

One day Wynn was in a pub when a Negro came out of the toilet. He did a double take. It was Winston.

"Winston you son of a gun!"

"Wynn!"

It had been a long time almost ten years. He worked as a roofer. He was drummed out of nursing by a the head nurse called Sparland, an authoritarian rat.

"Hey, you could a bin a good nurse."

"Yeah."

And down came the rain. Pitter.Patter.

One day the tutor called Wynn to his office and told him he was n't doin' very well and that maybe he'd chosen the wrong course. He held up an essay and said Wynn'd copied it verbatim from a book. Wynn said the course was badly organized, and had too much work for the students and that everybody copied each others essays as a result and left out adjectives to cover it up. The tutor paused but said nothing. He then said Wynn did not communicate very well with children. Which was true. The little swine got on his nerves. They would n't listen, and did n't want to learn. The tutor said nothing.

Down came the rain. And he went to bed with Judith Evans. She had indented nipples, and great wide hips with a puffy, comfortable mons venus, but they did n't fuck too well because she witheld from him because all the girl students could hear the noise through the chalets of the student village. And the students went off to get school teaching jobs while the tutor failed Wynn and he was left broke in a bedsitter. And down came the rain. Pitter. Patter.

These were bad days. He was holed up down the docks with a bunch of unemployed students. Sybil was still around. She had a boy friend with a gravel voice like Louis Armstrong and a fat gut like Tony Galento.

Sybil brought down Petal to see him every Sunday with the boyfriend who was also a Calor Gas salesman. There were cylinders all over the flat. In fact Sybil had got her boy-friend to follow Wynn for weeks. One night in a pub an ugly lookin fucker picked a fight with him so Wynn stepped in with a left hook and the bloke just stood there ready to take it when Wynn was grabbed by a couple of his mates. That's how he first got to know the boy friend ol' gravel voice. The worse thing was watching ol' gravel voice takin' Petal and puttin' her on his shoulders and walkin' away like a daddy when Wynn was the daddy. This really hurt. Sybil was now taking revenge.

Paternal love was thwarted. This was the signal for violence. One night Wynn had a skinful of booze, and was walking down Wind street when four guys came toward him. He hit one, as he passed, straight in the gut. The guy went down. Next thing someone had punched him straight on the button. "Get him!" Someone said. Wynn ran and hid behind the wall of a derelict building. He could hear their voices as they searched for him but they went away. Next day he woke up with an aching jaw and an hangover. Money was really short. He spent his Giro in days. For two or three days he was out of money all together.

These were really bad days. Sybil's revenge was absolute. The sky turned grey and heavy like lead. Everything seemed to slow to a funeral pace. He drank heavily. Was consummed with self pity. The doctor gave him sleepin' pills and valium. The junkies in the pub tried to buy the valium. The doctor called him, and checked his prescriptions. The junkies were disgusted.

Down the dock an Indonesian murdered another Indonesian and time went by as before. Wynn took up his trumpet and memorized *Stars Fell on Alabama.* He played it outside Sybil's flat after stop tap. And she put her head out of the window, then he fell off the wall, and pissed off back down the docks. When he was broke he started to write a novel called *The Love Story of Billy Llywelyn.* He wrote down all the hallucinations he had with the valium and the sleepin' tablets. He carefully wrote his sensations and built a story around his experiences in the mental hospital. It was all done in long hand in an accountant's ledger, then he put it on an Olympia portable typewriter. Maybe I can make some money, he thought.

One day he met Winston in the boxing gym – Wynn used to go down the boxing club to punch a few bags. He was very fit. Winston was fucked up with sugar diabetes and used to take injections once a day or was it twice. Winston was a middle weight while Wynn was six one and weighing fourteen stone. Winston had fought for the Welsh middle weight title, and had travelled around with the Jaylor's Fairground Boxing Booth, a very famous institution.

In the ring Wynn hit Winston with a left jab he'd been practising. Wap! Wap! Winston blinked. Wynn felt a little sorry for Winston. This was too easy. And this was the last time he was allowed to think at all. Winston hit Wynn with an old fashioned straight left, a straight armed punch delivered with full body weight that drove his head back against the ropes – the punch did not hurt. Then Wynn felt his body shakin' up as body punches smashed against his ribs in a tattoo, then Winston switched a left hook to the chin in a classic combination which exploded in his brain. Wynn's arms dropped and Winston stood back.

"Are you OK?"

"Let's go again," said Wynn, his fitness carrying him into involuntary lunacy.

"Punch!" said Winston.

Wynn swung but Winston went into a bobbin' and weavin' routine, swivelling his body on his heels and the balls of his feet. The punches got nowhere near. Once more Wynn was on the ropes with Winston hammering at his body. Wynn put both arms on Winston's shoulders and pushed him off halfway across the ring, and climbed out of the ropes like a scared rabbit.

"Fuck this," he said, tearin' off his boxing gloves.

The whole thing took less than a minute.

"You gotta punch more and move. You're too static. You wanna learn to get off those ropes. And I was pullin' my punches."

"Bollux."

Wynn's jaw hurt and his ribs were on fire. He felt sick. And his fear of Winston was intense. This was his nemesis.

"You'd better come back with us," said Winston's wife, a harpie from Ponypridd with two children by her first man and three from Winston. She was always ballin' at the stewards about exploiting her coloured husband who was deaf, a fuggin' good job as far as he was concerned. That night they went to a club – the steward hid in an alcove behind the bar. And Winston sang his Ray Charles number. Afterwards, they went home and Winston said: He'd better sleep with me 'cause he's 'avin a nervous breakdown."

Wynn took his sleepin' tablet and his valium and hallucinated a bit. Halfway through the night he felt Winston's black dick nudging his asshole, and got out of bed.

"You ain't fuckin' me Winston," he said, "you beat the fuck ouda me, but you an't fuckin' me an' all."

Winston just turned over and went to sleep. In the morning his wife knocked on the door. Bang! Bang!

"Why is this door locked? What's goin' on in there?"

Whad a mess? thought Wynn as he walked around the park, weeping like a baby with a painful sty on his eye. Whad a fuggin' mess! I gotta ged ouda o' this somehow. And his ribs were still on fire with a pain down his arm an' all and his kidney area seemed to throb like a cut finger. Was this his nemesis? The beginning. The end. Over the the park the sun rose in the sky, and a bird sang someway off, thinking it was spring time and started to build a nest.

Wynn had to ged out of the embrace of Winston and the Harpie so he got another bedsit.

"Whad are you pissin' us about for," screamed the Harpie on the phone.

This was a very bad time. He was unemployed. He was homeless. He was thwarted. He had offended the gods. He felt sick. He wrote his story. He read boxing magazines. He went and saw Mohammed Ali lick George Foremen. He wept. He had his hallucinations. He quarrelled with Sybil who ran away with his daughter. His daughter cried her eyes out for toys he could n't afford. He slugged an Irish guy in a pub for saying he'd smash Wynn's face in. He hit him so hard he staggered back ten yards into a bunch of drinkers when all hell broke loose and Wynn ran out the back door. All the women he approached rebuffed him. He stank of failure. He thought failure. He drank failure. This was his nemesis, his beginning, his end!

One day he smet Sybil's boyfriend on the bus, ol' gravel voice. They had a chat. Ol' gravel voice told Wynn about Petal, little tit bits of information that a father would tell someone. Wynn flushed. He was plenty mad. The guy was a just an ordinary bloke who'd separated from his wife. He just did n't know what he was saying. The bus went on. O1' gravel voices's name was John.

"So long, John," said Wynn and went to see his mother.

"Let her go," said his mother, "she's no bledy good anyway. She's bledy hopeless as a housewife. Bledy hopeless."

She emphasised the word hopeless like she emphasised every word she got a hold of and then she spun a web around the word.

"Bledy hopeless. The bledy kid, don't eat properly I was told. A hopeless bugger like that can't cook. Never once, when she came up here, did she offer to do anything. Bledy hopeless. Wynn, you're better off out of it. I have never seen such a hopeless bugger as 'er.They say she does bugger all but read. Her head's in a bledy book all the time. Hopeless. Bledy hopeless. That's the way they are today. Hopeless."

His mother put coal on the fire — she had plenty of coal from the coal board deal, and it came with the pension.

"Bledy hopeless bugger. You should 've married someone like me. I can bledy look after the house and clean it like a pin. That bugger's got no pride at all. Bledy hopeless. Her father's house was clean as a pin. Where the 'ell has she come from, then? No bugger knows. You are travelling everywhere and you don't know who your're pickin up in these bledy pubs. She's bledy 'orrible. Bledy hopeless, and bledy useless."

She put more coal on the fire. The fire spluttered. Dust

floated up and settled on the brass candlesticks.

"Here's five pounds," she said, "don't piss it against the wall. Bledy hopeless. When are you comin' again?"

"In a fortnight."

"Yes, that's right. Bledy hopeless."

And all his childhood flashed before him, and he held her hand again on Pontwalby Bridge, waiting for the bus to Rhigos Halt. And watched her make blackberry tart in the darkness of the kitchen as the wind swayed the trees of the Halt and far in the distance he heard the train's hooter so long ago.

And he got on the bus at Hirwaun and went back to Castell Blodau to the misery of bedsits and frustrated paternal and filial love and Sybil's anger. An ol' gravel voice got on the bus. He was pissed as newt, legless, and maudlin', almost unable to speak. Whad a fuggin' laugh. Legless ol' gravel voice stoned oud of his mind. They went for a drink. He salivered. He farted. He nearly fell over. He swayed. He dribbled.

He took out his money and tried to count it and failed. Wynn thought: I could knock him out with a left hook here. He would n't see it comin'. Blat! But he could n't. The guy was just a workin' guy probably under a lot o' pressure with his gas cylinders and Sybil, also an estranged wife to contend with. So Wynn just left him in the pub without even sayin' goodbye not that the guy would 've noticed. The last impression was a pathetically drunk bloke tryin' to count his money.

Gas cylinders are made from steel billets at forging temperature and placed in a 2000 tonne press, and pierced. The billet is drawn in a mandrel while neck is closed and the cylinder oil quenched and tempered. In every process, except in nationalized industries, surplus value is stolen by the capitalist class. In Castell Blodau, a run down dock town you will not find any representatives of this class. Castell Blodau is a proletarian town immortalized by Dylan Thoms whose characters patrol the ghostly streets they would no longer recognize O Sybil! Dylan Thoms did n't have a clue about Marxist surplus value. He celebrated the mystical qualities of language as revolt, *l'art pour l'art*. Over the Bristol Channel the sun goes down and the moon rises over the tide-woven sea, O Lord.

Wynn went down the university with the five pounds, and got well healed. When the barman came round and hit him in the face he never saw the punch comin'. Thwak! Wynn turned and hit the punk with two punches. The next thing he knew he was on the deck with a sharp pain in his chest and was unable to move. He never knew how that injury came because the mind had blanked it out forever just like leaving the camp had been blanked out forever so long ago.

"Take 'im away," said the barman with contempt.

Wynn was taken to the hospital and ex-rayed. He had a bruised cartilage just below the sternum. Like Jack Dempsey once said: in a fight anything can happen. He lay up in his bedsit and could hardly move for ten days as the knives of the nemesis threaded the nerves of his chest and vultures pecked at his liver.

Over the Bristol channel the sun goes down and the sands beneath the salt sea shift. The stars in the sky stay in their constellations emitting light photons, stars that seem so near you could touch them.

Far in the limitless sky cumulus clouds stretch carrying a thousand tonnes of ice awaiting the emission of rain over the crow's undulating flight in the fields of Castell Blodau.

———0o0———

6

RHIGOS HALT: 1948

The train blew its whistle through the tunnel near the Halt. He heard the sound a lot and he loved it. Bloot! Bloot! went the train. And Bloot! Bloot! echoed Wynn. There was another sound he loved and that was the sound of the river. Tinkle! Tinkle! went the river.

"Go and get some eggs," said his mother.

And he went along the road to Ann's small holding. Ann put the eggs in a brown bag. The eggs were covered in chicken shit and straw. On the way back he looked at the little streams that wended through the fields. He noticed they did n't make as much music as the river whereas there was always something going on in the trees. Sunlight. Old nests. Wind. Hoar frost. The roots, too, looked like things that could walk. And the trunks were green with lichen. Sometimes they looked like soldiers on parade, sometimes like ghosts especially when the sun went down. He loved the trees.

"Good boy," said his mother, her apron smelling of flour,
"you got the eggs without breaking one."

That afternoon, when his father got home, his mother told him he'd got the eggs without breaking one.

"He's not totally useless then," said his father, black from coal dust.

And time went by as before.

Above the Halt was a big mountain with no trees, and not much colour except a dull green and grey. The mountain seemed like a huge shadow over the Halt. Over the mountain was the Rhondda valley where his daddy had come from. His daddy told him some stories of when his daddy was a kid. How somebody stole his whinberries, and how he smothered the bloke's face with them, of huge fairgrounds with bearded ladies and very fat men. And of boxing booths. And people dying in the mine.

In fact when his father did n't come home from the mine Wynn's mother got a little anxious. She said nothing, but he could feel it emanating from her. On evenings like this she sat by the light of the flickering oil lamp twisting the ring on her finger, and sighing at intervals, but nothing ever happened. His father always came home smelling of coal dust with his pit boots and his grub box at his side. He'd worked a doubler or double shift, except one day there was an explosion but his father was not part of it. There was just a lot of talk about it that's all. His father had a brother who died in a mine blast, and his father said it killed Wynn's granny, it being her youngest son.

And time went by as before.

Wynn's father made him a rifle out of a zinc pipe which he attached to a rifle butt shaped out of wood. For a trigger there was a broken mug handle. It looked very real. Wynn ran along the river with it and hid behind little ant hills shouting Bang! Bang! Got you you buggerin' Jap! You buggerin' German! One day his father told him they had just taken a man to Sam's farm across the river because the man had put his arm on the rail and under the train's wheels' blat! Wynn sneaked down to the forbidden rail track to see if there was some blood on the rail but there was none. Sometimes Wynn stood on the bridge and let the train's steam pass over him and smelt its warm moist aroma. At other times he went to Sam's small holding and watched Sam at work with thc cows, and he went in the barn and played with the hay, or watched Sam mow the fields with his machine and his dray horse. And Wynn sat on the machine when it was idle and was mezmerised by the gold and red designs. At other times he got milk for his mother, and they gave him home made butter sandwiches. He loved Sam Bach because Sam never told him off about anything, and he played happily in Sam's fields.

There were all sorts of wonderful flowers in the fields, daisies, and clover. And down by the stream there were yellow marshmallows, and in the wood bluebells. Sometimes he could see little sand gobi fishes, ugly little dark brown things in the shimmering water. Wynn ran along the streams and the river. And he climbed the trees. One day they had a plague of frogs. There were huge frogs everywhere especially in the coal house. They were a luminous brown against the coal. And there was a war on in Europe. One day his uncle Davy came and played with him. He was on his uncle's back wow! gee gee wow! and his uncle went away to war and never came back. He lies to this day under the sands of Lybia.

Then his father went away to war, and came back with a rifle that went click! clack! And chased his mother round the kitchen with the bayonet and she giggled. Then his father came back to work in the mine because they needed coal. One christmas his father came home pissed dribbling from his mouth in the bed and his mother left him only to return later, and Wynn saw his father sitting beside the oil lamp sewing his pit clothes and he got up on his father's lap and kissed him, he smelled of cigarette smoke. Wynn then went to the cupboard and took out his ludo and snakes and ladders together with his christmas stocking that had oranges and nuts and a bar of wartime chocolate in it. There was a fishpaste bottle at the corner of the cupboard and Wynn said: “What's that there for Dad?” “To catch the bloody mice,” said his father.

And then his mother and father started to argue in Welsh and she drummed her fingers on the table cloth, and Wynn mimicked his mother, and his father told him off for it.

And time went by as before under the moon.

Wynn went down to Glynneath with his mother lots of times on the Western Welsh bus that throbbed and throbbed with its windows rattling. They went to Auntie Rose Owens and they had conversations over tea and biscuits, and Rosie always gave Wynn at least a thrupenny piece and a penny. And they stood on Glynneath square waiting for the bus in the cold, and walked down the long winding road to Rhigos halt. His father never seemed to be present. One day they went by train to Glynneath and there was a woman on the train dressed in black, and she took out what seemed to Wynn an enormous white breast that sent a shiver down his loins. That night an American sailor took out all his change and gave it to Wynn. There was seven and six, a lot of money.

“You’re a lucky little bugger,” said his father.

The sailor was out of Pennsylvania and was related to his father. Wynn's granny, his father’s mam, had emigrated and left a son by her first dead husband. She came home without him. She must’ve had a lot of babies, thought Wynn. One day a parcel came from America with the funnies and some candy.

“Look, he loves the comic,” said his father.

America was a long way across the Atlantic. And Wynn drew a big ship with a German submarine lurkin’ in the sea beneath it, and lots of fishes.“He’s a bloody good drawer,” said his father, and went off to work when the moon was out and the sky was dark. “He’s workin’ nights,” said his mother.

And Wynn slept next to her wide hips, warm as toast.

And time went by.

Through the woods and over the hill Wynn’s mother went to church with Ann. Wynn’s mother loved the church, but Wynn’s little bum felt uncomfortable on the wooden pews, and though he liked looking at the altar and the eagle of the apocalypse he was bored by the vicar because he understood very little.

One Xmas his father followed his mother to the church and sat in the back with his hat off. Wynn kept lookin’ at his father but his mother was seething madly about his appearance. Next thing Wynn remembers is his father following them home through the woods pissed as a newt and falling on the rough tones of the unmade drover’s road. Wynn went back to pick him up but there was blood drippin’ copiously from his nose.
Wynn’s mother said:

“Leave the drunken swine alone.”

One day his father brought home a lovely radio. He’d gotten it from the factory above the Halt on the moorland beneath the mountain. His father told him that he and Will Wing had got the radio from a loading bay, and that someone had hid it there so as to steal it, but he and Will Wing had beat ‘em to it. It was a beautiful radio and Wynn listened to “Dick Barton Special Agent” on it. And Valentine Dial as the “Man in Black.” Real creepy.

"Bloody good stuff," said his father.

His father liked the radio a lot. He was a fight fan. One morning he shouted up the stairs that Joe Louis had beaten Billy Conn. Later, Wynn’s mother went to work in the factory and brought home cakes from the canteen where his Auntie Glenys was workin'. Wynn was left in bed on his own when his father worked nights and his mother went to work early. They left a little lamp burning for him until stones struck the window and he went down to let his black father in with his grub box and pit boots.

Sometime later a load of Yankee soldiers came to the Halt and were camped in the woods.

"Don't go near them Yanks," said his father, nevertheless he went up to woods and they were camped there OK. A yank sitting on the grass with other soldiers said to him.

"Go and get some bread for us, kid, from the farm," and the soldier gave him a cube of sugar wrapped up in paper. And Wynn ran home and forgot all about the bread. Much later the Yanks moved out and they threw gum at him for opening the gate. His father had taught him to shout:

"Any gum, chum?"

"They were waving bars of chocolate, but they made sure they did n't throw them to you," said his father, bitterly.

Sometime later the sky was filled with aircraft droning in the sky with a myriad blinking red and white lights.

His father with his ear to wirless said:

"We've invaded Europe."

His mother wept beside the lamp.The trains in the halt hissed with steam, and they built a signal box beside the railway. And Wynn's father killed a snake by the river, and all the men building the signal box applauded him. Then Wynn was picking flowers down by the railway on a hedgerow and a thing hissed at him and he dropped the flowers and ran all the way home a fast as his legs could carry him.

And time went by as before.

Up on the factory estate there were bullet testing ranges. Crack! Crack! went the rifles, and Wynn went up there one day and played in the sand collecting spent bullets and his trousers split and he ran home ashamed of his nakedness.

On another occasion he was walking home with his father when they looked over toward a tent with a brazier outside in which a fire was smoking. Beside the brazier lay the figure of a man in police uniform, and the man was dead.

"You stay here," said his father, and went to get some other policemen.

Wynn looked at the man, his face was very pale and his lips were drawn over his teeth, and one of his teeth was gold. In Glynneath his father took off his cap and went to the funeral. His mother took Wynn to Rosie Owens.

Later his Uncle Shonni came to the house on the Halt and built a forge there because Shonni was a blacksmith. Shonni shoed the local farm horses and made iron hoops for Wynn's cousins who came from Bristol and spoke with funny accents with lots of umz and arz. Shonni also made a pig's bladder and blew it up with his forge bellows, and they all kicked it around. And Shonni disappeared with his wife who was Wynn's mother's sister, because Wynn's mother shouted at her. And Wynn started to go to school in the shadow of a mountain.

It was a long way and he had to cross the main road down which coal trucks passed. And one of the kids in the school got killed by a coal truck and the kids had a minute's silence. And Wynn went down the cellar of the house, it was once a pub – and wound up his record player, and he played Bing Crosby's *If you Ever go Across the Sea to Ireland* over and over. And he loved the music and memorized all the words.

And Wynn noticed that not all the people of the Halt

were friendly, in fact Mr Bulwell next door never spoke to his father nor his mother which seemed very strange. Only once did he venture into their house. They lived in the kitchen which was below the level of the front room, a dark and gloomy place.

Mr Bulwell worked on the railway, and had an immaculate garden. Wynn usd to look at it through`the inverted railway sleepers that separated the gardens. The reason why he went to Mr Bulwell's is that they had a niece come there, and he went into the house with her. Her name was Monica. Monica played with Wynn in the fields and she was taller and older than him and one day she put her arms around him and said he was a lovely little boy. But she stopped coming for some reason and he found himself playing on his own.

Then Mr Bulwell and his wife left. They went to England said his mother where they originally came from and another fellow came to live there. He was more friendly and sat in the doorway reading comics which was a very funny thing to do for a grown man.This man that read comics had a big black labrador dog and Wynn played with it all day in the fields, wrestling and trying to ride its back.

One day the Whipperin' came over the bridge, the Whipperin' wanted to know why Wynn never went to school. His mother said she'd see to it, so Wynn had to go to school everyday for awhile. The Whipperin' looked an important man with a big white moustache and a briefcase. Wynn's mother said the man came all the way from Neath because Wynn was a naughty little bugger who did n't want to go to school.

One day his mother and father took Wynn to the big mountain overlookin' the Halt, and they started to walk over it to the Rhondda Valley. It took a long time and they stopped lots of times for a rest. On the other side of the mountain there was a valley so beautiful it took his breath away. When they got halfway down the road they took a path down the hill, and Wynn's father stopped at a house and threw his cap in. He said if his cap came out he was n't wanted in that house, but cap did not come out so his father walked in and was embraced by a big woman with a grin and white hair and a sonorous voice. They were half brother and sister Her name was Gwen, and Wynn called her Bopa Gwen. He also had an uncle Trevor who was divorced from his wife. Uncle Trevor lived with Bopa Liz. They all had beautiful sonorous voices that reminded him of warm summer wind and the fragrance of clover. Bopa Liz called him bâch with a long vowel "e" instead an "a". And she sat by the fire in her apron.

Wynn's father, Idris, told Wynn that his grandfather was called Hywel. Hywel was in the great industrial confrontations of the Rhondda valley: the fight against the Cambrian Combine the homeland of the *Miner's next Step* who saw the unions as corrupt and the Labour Party opportunist.

"There are too many unions," he'd said, after coming from an Industrial Syndicalist League Education class, "we've got to carry on the fight inside the unions and take over the mining industry lock stock and barrel."

Later, Lenin said propaganda and agitation in the Trade Unions is essential to revolution:

TRAIN EDUCATE ENLIGHTEN

Over the Rhondda the sun went down, over the hills and the hill's streams. And Hywel's dream faded as the bourgeois politicians prevaricated in the bourgeois parliament, prevaricated and betrayed the socialist cause with jingoism.

(Troops and police were everywhere gunning down workers directed by a fat aristocrat who stank of cigars and brandy with a face like a baby. In the cinema's gloom children of the miner's booed his presence and Wynn joined in Boo! Boo!)

Hywel with a gammy leg through a mining accident had become a billiard hall caretaker beneath the cinema where Wynn viewed a film he was too young to understand.

And time went by as before, and down came the rain over the cinema's face.

Idwal sat in the tin bath washing, soap on his enormous bollux while Bopa Gwen with her white hair and sonorous voice that reminded him of summer wind and the fragrance of clover boiled more hot water and poured it into the tin bath. In the arm-chair next to the fire sat Idwal's father smoking a pipe. And later Wynn fell asleep in the warm bed on the never to be forgotten second floor until dawnlight filtered through the chintz curtains.

The mountain overlooking the Halt was never the same again. He knew what was over the other side of it, more mountains and rivers, and the moon high in the sky, and Gwen and Idwal and Liz and Trevor. And from his Bopa Gwen, every Christmas came a two and sixpenny postal order and a bag of sweets.

Into the Primary School came a German boy with leather trousers and leather boots. He was afterwards known as John German, and Wynn asked John German what the German name for father was and John German said "vater". And Ha! Ha! shouted the boys linking the noun with the English verb "to fart". And the headmaster of the Primary School clipped the boys round the head. The headmaster did a lot of clippin' round the head. A clip meant a heavy Smack! or several heavy Smacks! that sent the boys reeling. John German caused a lot of trouble, they thought.

The boys played cigarette cards against the wall and Wynn won a lot, and lost a lot. He played lorries around the yard Brmm! Brmm! shuffling his shoes along the earth. One day he drew on the school drain pipes with a red crayon and was clipped until he wept tears and was left in the yard all on his own to clean it off and he watched the workmen building a new school canteen in the next field. In the canteen the school held a prize day on which pupils were given books but Wynn did n't win anything and he figured it was because he was n't in school much.

On the Farm above Sam's called the Castell two tramps used to work, one was called Charlie and the other called Hugh. When you said "Hello Hugh". Hugh said: "yn y pink." Charlie said nuthin' to anyone. One day Wynn saw Charlie washing in the river, and Charlie put his soap in a clean sock. Wynn thought it was odd since Charlie had no socks at all on his feet.

Wynn liked to box in the school yard and had a good left with which, when he got in range, punched the other boy's on the nose. Wynn thought he was tough until one day Morton Jones punched him hard on the cheek bone. It was the hardest blow he'd ever experienced even harder than the headmaster's and he went around saying: "I'm gonna get Morton Jones," but he never did. Down by the river lived Rhiannon Thomas and Wynn was caught by the other boys picking crab apples with her. Rhiannon had ginger hair and all the boys teased him. "You're in love with Rhiannon Thomas!" And he challenged 'em all to box except Morton Jones.

And time went by as before. And his father went to work. And Ann took her eggs to Hirwaun on the train. And down came the rain. And across the sky sailed the moon.

Wynn was always avoiding his father who, as well as working in the mine, carried the post, and often walked through the factory estate which had ceased to make bullets now the war was over. Wynn used to be taken for rides in a lorry by a fellow named Joe who was Irish, and Joe had once taken him into the factory toilets – a lot of factories had ceased to work after the war and were vacant. In the toilets Joe sat on the loo seat with his trousers down and then he took Wynn's trousers down and got him to sit on his lap. Joe started to pull Wynn's willie and Wynn felt little butterflies in his bum. "Stop it, Joe!" he said. "Stop it!" because he got scared, and Joe stopped.

One day he was in Joe's lorry with a lot of other kids when he saw his father walking along so he hid under the dash board. Joe said nothing. Then a while later one of the kids slammed the door and caught Wynn's finger in the hinge which nearly took the top off. Joe got hold of Wynn's father and they all went to the doctor's who bandaged the finger up. "You're lucky you've got the top of your finger," said the the doctor. And Joe and his father went for a drink in the pub afterwards and Wynn had lemonade but his finger throbbed like a steam engine. That was the last time he ever saw Joe.

And time went by.

In the council houses above the Halt lived Will Pregethwr and Bessie, his wife. Will told his father that Wynn had stolen all the gooseberries from the one gooseberry bush in the garden. "Did you?" asked his father. "No, I did n't," said Wynn. "Will Pregethwyr is a miserable bugger," said his father. Evan Jones lived in one of the houses and Evan's father played Rugby for Wales and had caps in the drawer, they were red with silver tassles. He went North and the women up there hit him with their umbrellas cause he was a dirty player said his father. Wynn had a fight one day with Clive Huxley and Huxley never hit back. "Hit the bugger back," said Huxley's mother through the window, but he never did. Wynn used to watch Evan in the hot water bath covered in soap. Wynn was fascinated because he did n't have hot water down the Halt, nor a toilet that flushed.

And the days went by one after another.

The council houses were on the edge of moorland that ran to the mountain, and down in front of the houses the land sloped to the distant river. The river was surrounded by trees. The land-scape in front of the houses was mysterious and beautiful. The moorland seemed vast and ugly under the mountain. On the moorland was the factory with its avenues. The factory seemed a desolate place and you never saw the people except when they came out of the factory. They looked pale and tired and went away, and then the place was deserted. And the factory had ruined the river which was grey with scum. He always passed the factory as quick as he could and was always glad to get to the Halt and the trees and the fields and the little streams and the polluted river with its sad music.

Wynford Morris was in Aberdare Grammar School and told Wynn what they did there like algebra and chemistry. Wynford's father was a captain and had some position in the factory. In fact they lived in wooden houses with drives that were built during the war. They were English and seemed better off than the people living in the council houses. All the Welsh people seemed to work in the mine. Wynn liked Wynford Morris a lot. One day in school they both put their arms around Rhona Wilkins an English girl who was rather beautiful. She was very good about it and they both sat there with their arms around her rather ridiculouly until Miss Morgan came in who had a very bad temper and used to throw chairs around. Miss Morgan lived in the Castell farm next to Mr Rhys.

One day Wynn's mother took him to Penderyn over the hill and through the woods. And they reached the church where his father had taken off his cap and prayed, and the road fell steeply from there into the village and the village nestled in the foothills of the Brecon Beacons. Wynn's mother took him to a new council house and she turned the taps on in the skullery, and the water flowed from the taps like sinews of silver.

"This is going to be our new house," said his mother. And Wynn understood that the house on the Halt was condemned. And the word *condemned* had a very sinister meaning but he did n't quite know what except it was a very bad word.

And Wynn did not remember leaving the Halt just like he did not remember leaving the Camp because it was all very painfull though he did n't know it at the time. He'd left all his friends there forever – thc man next door who read comics and the labrador dog and Ann with her teacosy cap and one tooth and Sam with his almond eyes and Mr Rhys Castell and Hugh yn y Pink and Wynford Morris and Evan and all the others: Auntie Rosie Owen, and the Factory with its avenues. And he had witnessed his first death, and his first fear and dread, the song of the trees, and the song of the river, and his first tentative love and his loss.

And he went to another school. And one day he put his pen on Eirwen's blouse – Eirwen sat in front of him – and the ink spread on her blouse as though it were a piece of blotting paper. Eirwen told the headteacher, a Mr Roderick, and he hit Wynn about the head Smack! Smack! Smack! until hot tears came to his eyes.

One day he went to Hirwaun and sat in another school to do his Eleven Plus Examination and there was ink all over his sums so he used his blotter a lot. Those were the days of ink-wells and pens and blotters. And he passed his eleven plus and was going to go to the Grammar School. And his mother said:

"Our Wynn's going to be a Doctor," and all the kids laughed and threw gravel at his mother's window and ran away.

And time went by as before in sunshine and in rain.

And Wynn no longer played alone as he did along the river and its tunnels, and the fields of the Halt because now he was surrounded by children and they were horrible to him. The kids found a nest at the opening to a quarry and they went to see the nest until one day there was nothing there.

"I saw 'im kill the yunkers," said a girl, "he cut off their heads with a slate."

"No, I did n't."

"Yes you did."

"No, I did n't."

"Yes, you did."

They had surrounded him against the fence and were pushing him, especially the girls, and this made it very difficult. "Get Gwrth," they shouted. Gwrth came. He was small yet powerful and walked with long strides like a jungle cat, he sort of loped. He got Wynn by the lapels and said.

"If you killed those yunkers we gonna kill your cat."

Wynn was pretty scared and thought he was goin' to faint but he did n't instead he felt a surge of hatred come up in him and he thought Gwrth must've felt it because he seemed to melt away. It was the girls who grabbed his cat and took it into Gwrth's garden and threw it high against the wall.

"Yawl! Yawl!" went the cat trying to claw the higher part of the wall, and ran off.

One night under the lamplight Wynn put on the boxing gloves with Gwrth and Gwrth rushed at him and hit him hard because Gwrth was very strong.

"Fuck this said Wynn," and took off the boxing gloves, but he knew he could whip Gwrth with a straight left. He was scared of Gwrth because Gwrth showed an inner violence that was born of frustration, and repression. He was not physically scared of Gwrth but worried about something he did not really understand. This inner violence.

Gwrth was tough. He had a reputation. Who was Wynn to disturb the situation?

The kids went down to the river and built a damn and dived in the water. It was not very deep. The water was cold from the hills and made their bodies blue so they built a fire and stood around it shivering with towels across their shoulders and their legs turned red with fishnet patterns.

One day they were looking for trout and Wynn put his hand under a stone and got hold of one and held it until he could get it out. It was quite a large one and had a silver belly with roses on its side, and he took it home and his mother cooked it.

On another occasion Wynn pointed his airgun at a bird with a yellow breast, a chaffinch of sorts. The pellet hit the bird in the throat. It coughed blood, fell over and died. Wynn felt a terrible shame at killing something so beautiful that he never pointed his air gun at anything again except some crows passing by – they were ugly anyhow – much to his surprise the pellet hit the crow on the leg and its leg dropped as it flew.

Above the house was a wood full of hazel trees that had

once had kilns of a sort, maybe for making bricks, he was n't sure. Wynn and the kids loved to play there. They cut bows of briar or any other wood and made arrows of young hazel shoots. One day Wynn split the top of the arrow and put a chicken feather in it and secured it with cotton. He and another fellow stood on a small hill and shot the bow. The arrow sped away like a real arrow in a film.

"Jesus that's good!"

Penderyn was built on farming and the quarry industry. The quarry dominated the village and everybody worked in it except his father who still went to the coal mine. Penderyn meant in English, Bird's Head. It was a small village with white washed cottages at the foot of the hill on which the church stood. Next to the church there was pub called the Red Lion. It was said it was an old drover's pub.

In that pub his father had got drunk and had fallen on his nose on the way back to the Halt all those years ago. All his mother's family were in the village and her cousins, too. His grandfather had worked in the same coal level as his father, but later had become a quarry worker. He was long dead. His grandmother was still alive, but Wynn did not like her because she showed him little affection, indeed, it was the reverse, she always seemed to be criticising him. When she was ill he asked to sleep on the sopha so as to watch her die. One day he went in the room and she coughed and a trickle of blood seeped out of the corner of her mouth and she was dead. Cold as a stone slab. That was the second person he saw dead.

And time went by as the crows laboured across the fields.

One day his father said: "you come with me on the post and do some chores for this woman, and she'll pay some money to you."

He went to the woman who was English and she was small and dressed in black. She asked Wynn to trim the edge which he did then she gave him tea and biscuits and some money, and when his father came to pick him up he was very drunk because it was Xmas time and he had a drink in every house on his post round. The pit bus picked up his father and he was swaying in the doorway, and all the men laughed at him, and Wynn was very embarrassed and wished his father would n't get drunk so often. That was the last time he went to the Rhigos and shortly after his father gave up the post.

One day Wynn found himself in the Grammar school just like that. His parents bought him an uniform and a leather satchel. And then he went on a bus to Hirwaun and then on a train to Merthyr Tydfil and into Cefn Coed. And there were all sorts of different boys from all over the place. Some came from Pontneathvaughan which was in another valley. This was a new world, a big world, but the lamp still flickers over his mother's face in the dark and forms shadows on the rose-painted wall as darkness falls over the trees and the river: the Sand Gobi fish hides under roots of moonlit trees while through the house the winds blow over decaying slate, and crumbling mortar.

Love weeps in the moon-dark ruin.

—— 0o0——

7

CEFN COED GRAMMAR SCHOOL

Education has for its object the formation of character.

The teacher stood at the board with his academic gown flowing, chalking up algebra. Wynn wrote it down. It looked pretty with all those “x” ’s and “y” ’s and brackets, however, he understood little.

And time went by, but he was more conscious of its passing. And the leaves dropped off the trees in russet and in gold patterns.

In the science lab a teacher stood in front of the apparatus, in the apparatus a candle burned, and the water rose in the apparatus because the air pressure had been reduced due to the oxygen being used up by the burning candle. He understood that.

One day a boy knocked over a bottle of chemicals — there was always a stink of chemicals in the chemistry lab, a rotten stink — and Dai ‘Chem’ Davies hit the shit ouda the kid, and this was the way he did it. He slapped him round the mug. Slap! Slap! and stepped back. The kid’s face flushed, but he was grinning through his tears. The teacher hit him again until he stopped grinning. Slap! Slap! All the class was shocked — pale and silent. After that the Wynn learned his chemistry by rote, a whole excercise book of notes. All the kids on the train were amazed.

“Let me look! Hey Wynn, start here, where it says *metals*.”

Wynn rambled on verbatim, every word locked in its

place, only thing was it had no meaning. He could not connect the part to the whole, but he could do something the others could not. Learn by Rote. However, he found rote was no good. So he dropped the idea. Too much hard work anyway. Of chemistry, of Maths he knew nothing. He tried agriculture. This was rote learning par excellence. The teacher stood there dictating notes until Wynn's arm ached. The word *potassium* kept coming up and disillusionment came creeping round the corner and hanging 'round in the shadows. "Blah! Blah! Potassium. Blah! Drone! Potassium." One day in maths he worked out a theorum on his own. He felt good, but it did n't last.

Rugby Evans had a good dick, and a girl friend, but he stuttered all the damn time. He seemed to get stuck on "p" 's. And it was puh puh puh puh most of the time. So the teachers gave up asking him questions. Now because Rugby Evans had a good dick he would take it out in the train a lot. It was very thick but not too long. He measured it with a ruler. It was six and a half inches.

"That's my . . puh . . puh . . puh . . puh . . . prick ok" he said.

Another thing Rugby Evans did was to cheat. He cheated in exams by putting his excercise book on his knees beneath the desk and copyin' out the answers. The answers were irrelevant to the questions, naturally, but this was not the point, Rugby was participating in the grammar school system.

What relevance did algebra and Latin have to Rugby Evans whose father was a miner, and nasty bugger to boot, brutalized by conditions, willing to fight at the drop of a hat, always doin' the pools with a pencil behind his ear at least whenever Wynn was in the house? And every home has an atmosphere and this particular house did not seem to welcome visitors and this atmosphere came from Mr Rugby Evans who seemed cold and slightly threatening at the table doing his pools. This cold rather threatening manner of his made Rugby Evans Jnr stutter in terror as a child. Maybe. Maybe not. Anyhow Rugby Evans was a very sensitive teenager with a beautiful physique, but there was no nastiness in him, nor any violence.

"Hundred lines boy," said Happy. Happy Lewis was the maths teacher. He had discipline problems 'cause nobody understood algebra except the twins who sat in the front. Happy was always dishing out lines. A hundred lines of

"I must improve my discipline in class, starting now," or some other epigrammatic gem as written down in fragments falling across the page, filling up space "I must

I must

I must improve"

ET CETERA

Slap! Slap! Quiet boy! Get out! get out! And time went by with Latin, English Grammar, English Literature, Chemistry, Biology, Physics and fights . . .

Wynn is in the middle of the playground with his antagonist, a Shonni Jones. He is boxing well using his left just like he did in the primary school and under the street light with Gwrth. Boxing is an art, a science, a manly sport watched by tens of thousands. Shonni bulls-in, head down, and is so easy to hit. All the kids are screaming in a circle. Suddenly the bell goes and the teacher spoils everything. But Wynn has won the boxing match. He has a few bruises mostly on his knuckles, but he has won on points though he is not the toughest in school. Dai Thomas is. Dai is real tough. His brother is doing time for manslaughter in Swansea jail so it's said. Dai is bigger than anyone, bigger and stronger with big hands and very nasty. He is big as Rugby Evans and twice as nasty. Dai likes Wynn for some reason because Wynn has a way of just observing people without antagonizing them.

And time goes by in the rain and the sun of schooldays.

"I don' wanna go to school," Wynn shouts from the warmth of his bed.

"Stay bledy there then," says his mother.

It's the same as Rhigos Halt, his mother don't care if he goes or not. She's got something against school. She's got some kind of attitude. No wonder with all that Latin and geometry an' algebra thinks Wynn. Anyhow he likes it in bed. It's warm and comfortable while outside the rain comes down and washes the green trees in the wood opposite. This is what he loves. The wood with its little darknesses, with its loamy smell, and its cathedral of leaves. The wood that could at any moment become anything — a battlefield, a sea of ships, a kingdom of thieves and pirates.

"If you got the bikes," he said to Gwilym Finch "I got some money from pop bottles."

And off they went to Hirwaun Miner's Welfare Cinema to see Errol Flynn, and some swashbucklin' stuff. They put their bikes in somebody's house 'til the show's over. The woods now awaits the enactment of the drama which has taken place in the cinema. A hill becomes a crow's nest, a hazel shoot a sword, a rope tied to a branch a boarding aid. Yahoo! Yahoo!

He has learned to be alone in the woods as it comes alive to the magic of imagination. One day he comes across the farmer who owns the wood, but the framer is partially blind, and Wynn hides behind a tree, still the framer senses someone is there and waits in eerie silence then turns away.

Ken 'Boney' Jones grabs Wynn in an arm lock and hits him three or four times with his fist in the mouth and nose. His lip swells and his nose bleeds. Wynn is badly hurt and shaken. This was not boxing, this was not science but brutality. He is betrayed. He hates 'Boney' Jones who he thought of as a friend — he'd taken him home and they put black lead on their shoes instead of polish. Silver shoed they walked through the village together before going to Boney's, three miles away over hills and valley's. Boney is a tough bastard, but not as tough as Dai Thomas. Wynn has misplaced his affection. He goes to show the teacher his fat lip, but the teacher laughs and makes Wynn sit in the deserted dining room to get over the shock. Wynn ought to get Dai Thomas to punch the shit ouda Boney Jones but he decides against it. You gotta fight your own battles.

Wynn is playing along the side of the lower quarry, (there are two in the village,) when Charlie Lloyd comes over the hill with two dogs. Charlie waves his stick and shouts. All the kids run away. Charlie Lloyd is nuts say the kids. Much later Charlie Lloyd is taken away to a hospital in the hills of Breconshire. The kids play unhindered along the quarry. Every spring come the rooks to their nests of sticks and feathers that fill the hollow recesses of the rocks. All the kids climb the steep slopes to the rock's face and peer at the scrawny-necked, bulging-eyed little horrors while mothers wheel and sqwauk in terror above the kid's heads.

And time goes by in the wood as the wood darkens towards the winters that pass into other springs, and into other summers.

And all this time Wyn's father goes to the mine, and comes home with a block of wood under his arm, and on Saturday night goes to the pub and gets bloto and sits beside the fire warming his hands and sometimes gobbing in it. Another thing he's always out of fags so he takes his dog-ends and puts the old dry tobacco in paper cut from the side of the *Daily Express* and smokes it. He's given up the post because its too much for him. He's gettin' on and asks Wynn if there's a bald patch on the top of his head so Wynn takes a look and surely there's a bald patch there and a dent in his father's cranium. "How'd you get that," says Wynn. "A stone fell on my head in the mine," replies his father. And Wynn turns on the radio his father stole with Will Wing and finds Willis Conover on AFN and is hooked on jazz music. "Bloody noise," says his father. One day Mr Rugby Evans knocks on the door and asks Wynn's father, Idris, about something. Mr Rugby Evans is looking for trouble but goes away. Wynn wonders what its all about. Nuthin' as usual.

Sometime later Wynn goes down the Youth Club and gives a lecture on jazz with the aid of a gramophone and some records. The Youth Leader commends Wynn to some body or another. Wynn is very proud of himself.

In school Rowley Jones is dancing with the French mistress in the gym. The French mistress has freckles on her nose and is beautiful like Virginia Mayo. All the boys note that Rowley's got an hard-on. Miss Owen walks down the corridor and Wynn gets an hard-on on account of her big breasts. She eventually marries the history teacher, a Mr Harries. Dai Thomas beats up a prefect and anybody else who cheeks him. The head teacher is a doctor but of what nobody knows. He's caned Wynn many times and Wynn always breaks down in front of him. There's a big controversy in school among the pupils about whether Sugar Ray knocked out Randy Turpin before the bell sounded.

And time goes by as before with chemistry, with biology, with agriculture and maths.

Happy Lewis is nuts as well as Charlie Lloyd. Happy plays the violin in the school orch and wags his head around with passion while playin' hymns. All the boys sing: "Put another nickel in/in old happy's cocoa tin/when he plays the violin/its murder, murder, murder..'

In Aberdare Park two school boys climb a tree and find a body below with twenty six stab wounds. The man is a Polack from the displaced people's hostel in Hirwaun. The local cops bring down Fabian of the Yard who fails to solve the case.

And time goes by.

In the Youth Club Wynn dances with a farm girl with big breasts and gets an' hard on : walks with her while all the boys ask what's the matter with him, but he's thwarted because her father comes down from the hills to accompany her home.

It is summer and there's the village fete. Wynn gets an idea and rubs his body with gravy brownin', puts a white towel round his shoulders, puts red ink on his eyebrow, puts on boxin' gloves and joins the fancy dress parade as Sugar Ray Robinson. He is stinkin' and cold with goose pimples all over his skinny torso. The prize goes to Mena Rodsborough the teacher's daughter dressed as a fairy, white dress an' all. Wynn is disgusted and curses the stupid judges.

Back in the grammar school Wynn tries to get the English teacher's attention because he wants to read from the "Ancient Mariner" by Coleridge but the English teacher, a moustachioed braggart, ignores him. He gets Dai Thomas to read instead.

And time goes by in the wood and his father gets sick

and goes to try to get national assistance but is refused and gets a lift home from the pub in a beer lorry. The beer lorry crashes on Hirwaun square and Idris comes home with a black eye and bruised knee caps and so his mother ups and leaves, again. She goes to a farm to a childhood friend and Wynn sleeps with her son under a sloping roof who's got dirty feet. After awhile his mother goes home and argues with her husband in Welsh and Wynn gets up from the table and punches a hole through the kitchen door made of plywood. They stop arguing and fuss over him as he breaks down in tears. There is always a shortage of money now his father don't take the post no more so he works in the pub doin' odd jobs and sometimes goes to Ann's small holding.

One day both his parents are in hospital and he goes to his aunts. While he is in bed his uncle comes home from the pub and climbs in bed beside him. He takes Wynn's hand and places it on his nob. His uncle's nob is hard as iron an hot as a poker and very big. He pulls his hand away and his drunken uncle falls asleep.

It is winter and the boys are whizzing down the slopes of the fields near the entrance to the quarry. They are going down on zinc sheets taken off old sheds at fantastic speeds. Wynn's father makes him a toboggan out of wood. It is shaped like a shovel and has two runners down the side with copper piping. Wynn pulls it along the road to the fields. Put in place at the top of the slope it does n't budge, but sticks in the snow leaden still. All three boys laugh.

Time goes by.

Wynn's uncle and Mr Rugby Evans have a fight outside

the pub one Saturday night. Mr Rugby Evans blackens his uncle's eye. Idris mimes their styles. Rugby Evans Snr carries his left very low while his right is cocked for action. Wynn's uncle fights from a crouch like Tommy Farr. Now Wynn has got nuthin' against Rugby Evan's Snr but he does fight in a funny way, besides he always has that air of menace and very often Mrs Rugby Evans has got a black eye. They say Mr Rugby is a jealous man. Actually one way or another there are a few fights goin' on especially on Saturday nights, but they all seem one punch affairs, knockouts in under two minutes in the opening rounds. Very often Wynn has a fight or two. He goes up to the farm where the squire used to live and boxes with Llyr Lewis. They, box with leather hedging gloves in the barn. These also are one punch affairs for whenever a punch lands in the chops the gloves are taken off to inspect the damage.

Rugby Evans Jnr has a brother called Patrick who is younger but nasty like his father. He is also big and rather stupid in that he always grins about this an' that which irritates Wynn. One day Wynn goes down the brass band and gets hold of a trombone. He tries to blow it but having no sense of rhythm he tries to play jazz on one or two notes. Da de Da blat! he goes. Patrick gets a set of drums and bangs fuck ouda them also with little rhythm. Wynn and Patrick sit in the front room and play records and jam. One day Patrick brings a girl up from the YMCA dance and she sits on the sofa gigglin' with Patrick who's got a good physique like his brother. Patrick lays there with his shirt off while he and the girl start to kiss. Wynn packs his brass band pea-shooter trombone stinkin' of brasso and goes home in disgust. Fuckin' stupid dame.

Wynn loses touch with school. His misunderstanding widens to a chasm. Happy Lewis goes too fast at maths.

Agriculture is a bore. The Latin teacher is a dope, teachin' them about battles. There's more interestin' battles in Penderyn wood after seein' Errol Flynn in Hirwaun cinema. Dai Chem's a bastard knockin' everybody about except the twins. The Headmaster's a prick who fancies himself a cricketer and spends his lunchtime in the nets with the sixth form bowlin' at him. The Welsh mistress has a fat arse, and is always in a temper 'cause nobody gives a damn about Welsh. Another thing some people disappear from school because they're ill. Next thing he hears is that they're dead. Wynn decides that the best thing to do is not a give a damn about anything so he writes cowboy stories instead and illustrates them with drawings. All the kids think his stories are wonderful. Wynn reads one to Dai Thomas who laughs and walks away, bemused. Dai definitely does n't understand Wynn because Dai can't seem to find an excuse to punch him and assert his authority.

And time goes by with bewildering speed.

One day Wynn makes a friendship with Iomi Beck. Iomi's ol' man is a Czech doctor and lives in a big house under the viaduct with an orchard. Wynn goes home with Iomi and leaves to catch the train with a satchel full of apples. "I hope you did n't steal them apples," says his father, smoking a cigarette cut out of the Daily Express newspaper. "Iomi Beck gave them to me, dad," said Wynn with pride. His father coughed and spat in the fire. But Iomi did n't stay long at the grammar school. Iomi gives his form teacher a present, and leaves. Goodbye Iomi Beck says Wynn to himself.

Wynn scores a try playin' rugby. Dai Thomas pushes his face into the ground and Wynn gets up with a mouthful of grass.

Dai is sent off ignominiously. Dai still does n't understand Wynn even though he's asserted his authority at last. You can't win with some people, says Dai to himself who's thinkin' about bein' a copper when he grows up.

And then there was Mr Parr, known as the Gnome because he'd got big eyes and even bigger pouches under them, He smokes Player's cigarettes all day. Cough! Cough! Now when the smoke gets in his eyes they water like two drippin' taps. Cough! Drip!/Cough! Drip! Mr Parr is the woodwork teacher. Under his supervision Wynn makes a coffee table and takes it home. His father says: "good table that." And spits in the fire. His mother puts it in the best room.

And time goes by with comical speed.

A fifth former lends Wynn a fountain pen for a test. Wynn loses the pen while playin' football in Coed y Gurnos, a playin' field with a ring of pine trees. When he goes to the school he tells the bloke who threatens him. Wynn spends hours snivelling over every blade of grass, and, much to his relief, finds the pen. Some people are really nasty, he concludes. Anyhow, he does n't sit the test. He's rarely in school. He prefers the wind in the leaves and the rain on the leaves in the wood, an' sleepin' an' dreamin' in bed. He prefers watching the flight of the crow, and the sparrows in the hedgerows and bicycling to Hirwaun cinema with money from empty Corona pop bottles with Hilary Finch's brother, Gobobimus, whom he loves. And every day Wynn's father goes to the mine, and works *doublers* and brings home the bacon and goes to bed and smokes his Woodbines, and reads his *Daily Express* and comes home Saturday night with flagons of beer — no drink on dry puritan

Sundays — in each pocket much to his mother's disgust. And in the morning holds his hungover head in his hands while his mother says "serve the bugger right." At these times Wynn discovers the toilet bowl is full of diarrhoa with a Woodbine in it. Flushes it and thinks what a bloody bloke his father is. All he does is work, and stagger home from the pub, also he's always on about *double partin's, traffic shift,* and cursin' the government.

And time goes by with bewildering speed.

Wynn goes down the track to Hirwaun and meets Georgie "Shush" Jones and his brother Russell. They're nastier than Dai Thomas, but twice as thick. Wynn says hello and scurries by like a rat up a pump wonderin' what they've stolen, looks back and runs. He calls at a cottage to see a school acquaintance. The mother opens the door and says the kid's not in. She's got beautiful breasts tucked in a black sweater. Wynn's young genitals tingle and his kness turn to jelly while he tries to catch his breath. "Jesus," he hisses to himself. He goes to see the twins who've a big terraced house over looking the ruins of an ancient iron works. Their father who smokes a pipe is an insurance salesman, a couple of steps up the social ladder from Wynn's father. In fact everyone he meets seems to be one step up from his father. I bet the twins ol' man is not always at work or pissed in the pub when he ain't gobin' in the fire. The twins are very glad to see him, but their pipe-smoking dad sends Wynn on his way since his boys have to study. Wynn does n't study anything, but walks around observing things he does n't quite understand.

O that woman in the cottage! O Jesus! O God! Them tits! He decides to go back along the railway track, but has n't got the courage to go back and knock on the door and gaze at her breasts. He just stands there at the bottom of the garden path in a trance until in the distance he hears the quarry train comin' down the track. Bloot! Bloot! Wynn hides in the hedge until it passes and goes home to imitate Errol Flynn in the woods.

And time goes by with beligerent speed.

And suddenly with time passing Wynn finds he's nearly sixteen. Five years of grammar school life has passed in a flash. Five years of observation and tears, five years of mis-understanding, and of non-understanding either chemistry or maths. Five years of long absences and five years of Dai Thomas, Boney Jones and the twins. Five years of Gwrth and helping on the farms spreading dung, lifting hay onto gambos, feeding the cows, and dipping the sheep. Five years of waiting and watching.

One day his father gets him an interview in the coal board area office for a position as an apprentice electrician. The interviewer is not sympathetic. Wynn is drifting in stormy hostile seas. What of his school certificates? None! What of his enthusiasm? None discernable in so young a dreamer. He needs help, sympathy. The bald-headed, tied, and suited engineer gives him nothing except cold efficiency and some suspicion. Wynn fails. His father now tries the screens in the washery, picking slag off the conveyor belts. Nothing. Wynn lands up in the limestone quarry with his ancestors. His father hides his disappointment and gobs in the fire, goes to work and comes home and reads his *Daily Express*. And time goes by as before under the moon, under the stars. And this was the last of Wynn's schooldays.

———0o0———

Trotskists know this, the Communist party chooses to ignore it. As long as wages are paid there is surplus value.

In the board rooms and in the political forums the capitalist class is waging its war against communism and the Soviet Union in the form of the Economic League with its "black lists" of agitators and militant traded unionists. The British Steel Corporation which belongs to the common working man utilizes these "black lists". Large banks contribute money to the Economic League. This money is stolen from their employees in the form of surplus value. There is an office in Cardiff, but it is not known if Wynn is on this list or not.

Through the streets of Castell Blodau Wynn carries the *Morning Star* to its subscribers. They are all poor and live in terraced streets and council houses on the ridges of bleak landscapes. The Morning Star is the only newspaper that belongs to the common working man and works in his interest. The Morning Star is sold all over the Soviet Union and Eastern Europe.

Across the street a woman gazes into the window and combs her hair. She is absolutely beautiful. Wynn's breath condenses of the windowpane. Sybil is in an education lecture.

And time goes by as before.

They are scrumming down in St Helen's, the steam of the heat of their bodies wafts up in the cold air. Wynn watches from the stand. There is some loose play, a maul forms and collapses. There is a crack. "It's gone, boys," says a player meaning his leg's broken. He is carried off. The game goes on. One of the Neath players is a Welsh international. Wynn has gone to school with him. Everybody seems to have achieved something except Wynn, but he's in there pluggin' away.

In the Steel Works they are playing a game called Black Bitch which revolves around the Queen of Spades. There's fuck all else to do. They play it all day and get into terrible tempers when things don't work out.

Llanelli: the rugby pitch is shrouded in mist. It is cold. In the distance there is a small hill you can just see through the mist. A crow flies over it. The atmosphere of the rugby match is electric. Wales are producing players of great ability and excitement. Wynn is fond of going to rugby matches and watching all the characters in the drama. He feels the start of something big and he's feeling like a married man struggling to raise a family. He feels a sense of importance.

Llanelly rugby team is called sospan since the town makes tinplate. Tin is expensive stuff running around £8,000 a tonne. It is corrosion-resistant. Tinplate is made from mild steel with 1/lOth carbon and rolled to 0.17 mm, coated by the process of electrodeposition. Church bells are made from tin and bronze for sonority. Ding! Dong! Ding! Dong!

Wynn had a nickname, long forgotten, from his grammar school days, laid on him by the schizophrenic twins. His nickname was stannus which is Latin for tin. This is because at Rhigos halt he lived in an old drover's inn called Tin Ton. The plot thickens. The rugby match ends, and Wynn catches a train back to Castell Blodau over the cockled mud flats. Long ago his grandfather came from Llanelly to mend hedgerows and became headteacher of a small school in Ystradfellte, a farming settlement in the foothills of the Brecon Beacons.

Now a hundred years later Wynn goes home to Sybil. He likes the contrast between the cold outside on the rugby pitch and the fire burning in the grate of the flat. He is young and full of energy, but work oppresses him. The filth of the Steel Works and the lack of prestige angers him. There is something missing from his life that he's unaware of except that it results in a form of misery. Ding! Dong! Ding! Dong! Beside him in the bed overlooking the street, suspended as though in air, Sybil weeps into her pillow. Wynn gazes at the ceiling. Sibyl also knows of misery, but it seems a different kind of misery.

What is this life about, thought Wynn, while sitting in the office of the Steel Co at one thirty in the morning, what is this life about? Is it about Sybil and her group? Is it about noise, cacophony and garbage? Is it about me? Me and my perception? Me and my trumpet? Can I change my life because as it is things are drivin' me nuts. Sybil is driving me nuts with her clumping around, with her ire, with her niff. I'm definitely on a journey that's half begun. Suddenly, he realized he was free. He could sell his labour at anytime to anyone. If that was what freedom was.

An image came to him of Violet against the gate, and the stars were in the sky. Her tongue was in his mouth licking his lollipop tongue. He had his hand in her nickers in the cleft of her dew-wet genitals. His cock extended six inches from his groin, longing for the red hot heat of her vagina. / O spongy thighs! O elastic vagina! O glans penis! O ecstasy! O trembling buttocks! O womb that winks in your eye! O Eros! O Aphrodite! O bark of fox in the wood where I played as a child! O moon over the Rhondda! O gate that rests her female loins! O.o.o.!!! And he shot his load in his trousers whoosh! slurp! wet and warm down his trouser leg.

"You look flushed," said a fellow night worker, "want a kip do you?"

— RAF Innsworth 1957. Eyes sleepy. Uniform chafing his legs. Fuggin' forces! O sleep! that scarfs the eyes, that bandages the eyes. Acrid cigarette smoke sucked into the lungs, bitter, nauseous. I am only eighteen.

And through the hundreds of thousands of tons of steel lattices he goes to clock out, tired, weary, his body clock thrown out of sic, through the hundreds of thousands of tons of steel lattices covered with zinc sheets that enclose the rolling mills, and rolling stock . . .

And he goes home to the woman in the window to her white form in the distant room, to her heavy, drooping, fleshy breasts, her thin upper torso, her shoulder length hair, her burgeoning hips: sneaking to the window in the damp air with an hard-on wanting to bury himself in her vagina. And when he was not looking at the woman the image of the oil lamp from Rhigos Halt came smoking with the smell of the oil from the burned wick wafting up through the glass, blackening the ceiling. And the reflection of the lamp in the window. And a shadow of a moth flitting over the lamp. And the absence of people, the utter absence . . .

* * *

The smel1 of sweat and the smell of leather gloves excites Wynn. He is lined up with the other boxers. A pudgy ex-soccer player, and a three-fight-pro-bum are in the ring. Wynn's so keyed up he goes in wailing with both hands. His opponent is confused, but clears his head, and moves out of range, but Wynn catches him with a long left hook right on the button, the kid is momentaryily hurt, licks his lips, throws a quick left into Wynn's face and moves away.

"That's enough," says the trainer. Then he puts in another boxer with Wynn. "Take it easy with him," he continues. Wynn moves around the ring, moving left then right.

The kid miss-times a huge right, and ends up over the ropes. "That's it," says the trainer. Wynn gets out of the ring and goes home. He's got an headache. He lies on the floor listening to *Louis Armstrong plays Duke Ellington.* He feels elated, elated and heroic. He is laying on the floor. Sybil looks down at him from her easy chair. She has a look of contempt on her face.

And time goes by as before.

Sybil and Wynn visit Wynn's monosyllabic and bi-lingual mother. She is sixty five and has white hair. Wynn's mother embodies the whole economic and social history of the village. She and her family has always been there even when it was three houses and a pub. She describes it in monosyllables. Wynn reads betwen the lines. Sybil takes it all in and realizes she's come down in the monosyllabic world instead of up. After a breakfast of fried beans and bacon they walk through the woods to Rhigos Halt. (Sybil is a great walker.) Wynn knows every tree in the way a town dweller knows every house and alley nuance. He knows every lichen-covered stone and singing brook, and every stone in the singing brook.

They call at Ann's small-holding. Ann is hunched over the fire with a tea-cozy hat on her head. She is dying. Wynn can tell somehow. It is the way she looks at him. She's had enough. It's in her eyes. In that thousand mile stare she's got like she's given up on life, seen everything and does n't want to see anymore. She's also uncomfortable with her visitors. She keeps staring into the flickering fire. Wynn notices everything is its place. The chaise lounge is still there under the window. The radio is on the table and the Welsh dresser is covered in plates against the wall opposite the fire. The mantelpiece with its brass candlesticks and mirror is still there. Wynn hears the loud tick of the clock, too, measuring time as time goes by in the music of the wind in the leaves outside and the stream running down from the silent hills. After polite conversation Wynn and Sybil leave.

It is the last time, he knows, he will ever see Ann with her tea-cozy hat, one tooth and a wart on her nose who walked three miles uphill through the wood every summer, and once at Christmas. Wynn's beginning to think that you return to the scenes of your childhood just once to see if the magic world is still there. Everything is in its place but the magic has gone.

Wynn and Sybil walk along the railroad track towards Hirwaun — they go back to Penderyn in a kind of triangle — while she gets a 'mood' on.These moods can last hours or even days. She's a very unhappy dame. And this unhappiness is expressed in the *mood.* The mood becomes a way of life because the mood gets your attention. She's developed the mood mode of existence. During the mode of the mood she lays on the floor stiff as a plank or hides in the bedroom or looks out of the window and weeps or throws little pathetic punches at him or enact some significant drama about what some man did to her that day.

The form the mood now takes on while walking the railway track is the *walking away* mode. And what effect does this have on the recipient but *concern* for the mood. What has he done for her to walk away? Wynn feels guilty. After all he's caused this mood. He's said something to make her react like this. He's bored her with his childhood memories. She's far too sophisticated for all this squalor, for this decay and death, rural dreams and monosyllables. And that is why she's walking away to punish him for his indiscretion and he deserves it.

"Are you alright," he asks, concerned, as he's trying to catch up.

"She's lonely," Sybil says, talking of Ann. Wynn takes this to mean that Sybil is lonely. How the 'ell could Ann be lonely? After all she's had a radio for forty years or more, and her chickens. Ah, well! Ding! Dong! Ding! Ding! And when they get back and sit in the pub Sybil gets a *resentment* against one of the quarry workers, a red-faced farmer's son from the foothills of the Brecon Beacons, oafish, and boisterous.

Wynn is not only concerned, he now feels resentment against the fellow with his stupid presence, half drunk and pot-bellied. After all the fellow must have insulted her in some way, but when? Wynn sits there in a gloomy mood eyeing the guy up for a left hook or something, maybe a head butt. You just can't relax. Dead mother! Dead brother! Wimp father! Horrible step-mother! Monsosyllabic mother-in-law! And a future beckoning one rung up the ladder. Wynn goes to the bar and eyes the drunk up. Wynn thinks: I am taller, more intelligent, and slimmer. He gets a drink. Sits down. He feels the alcohol hit him in the belly, cold and full of gas. Sybil still resentful. He is concerned.

Time goes by. Nothing changes. Down comes the rain outside. O resentment! O concern! O unhappiness! O dolour in the hinterland! She's beginning to form unhealthy ideas about the village like for one the PEOPLE ARE BACKWARD . . . . .

— the rain is coming down pitter-patter on the shed that houses the boiler. It is cold. The boiler heats the tar macadam in the tanks. Not only is it cold and damp but Wynn has the flu. All his joints ache. He has an headache and a bad cough. In fact when he coughs his eyes water — he drinks hot tea coated with residues of oil from the well, but he has to go back to his perch on the conveyor belt. The noise is horrific, crushers pound, a thousand stones rattle through the iron screen, stones crash on stones like symbols, drop forty feet into huge bins. BANG! CRASH! while dust hangs in the windless winter air. It is freezing up on the gantry. Wynn shivers. He is only seventeen, and gets half the wages of a grown man. Nobody takes days off with such things as the flu. You must suffer for wages. Wynn is transforming raw material into a finished product, coughing and spitting dust —

. . . he and Sybil are in bed in his mother's old age pensioner's bungalow shaggin' with ferocity. Sybil has an inordinate sexual appetite based on the neurosis of loss — dead mother, dead brother — hatred of father. But the neurosis has not yet fructified. Her niff is strong, body odour, vagina fish-smell. Shaggin' is good here. There is absolute silence in the landscape outside. The bed is warm. In a camp bed sleeps the child. Wynn's mother sleeps in the box room you could n't swing a cat in. Does she hear the bing bang and the creak of the bed? Does she hear her son perform his nuptials from her lonely bed? Bing! Bang! Creak! They don't seem to care. But what Freudian thoughts enter his mother's monosyllabic head lulled by the heat of the blankets?

Far off an owl hoots in the dark. Wynn lays on his back and thinks of the quarry, of how hard it was and of how hard it is now. How low in prestige are the workers. He can't understand why his wife, with her *resentmen*t, deems to look down on them.

He's tinged with the innocence of the village, of his boyhood, his early manhood which he carries like some kind of fool. These were the men who first asked him if he'd dipped his wick or if he saw a cunt he'd run home and tell his mother he'd seen a butcher's shop on fire. Men who'd taken his week's wages playin' brag, teased him and gave it back, who'd told him he'd got such a big *taw* that he'd been seen protectin' it with two hands while he took a piss. Men who'd looked after him, and teased him in appalling conditions of work . . .

Suddenly he was aware of the tick of the clock, turns over on his side with his limp, wet dick, prick, taw, chopper, and falls asleep in the niff of Sybil's body odour below the stuffed birds on the tallboy.

Morning. It is time to say goodbye and return to Castell Blodau on the shakin', bumpin', rattlin' Red & White bus to the flat overhangin' the street to the stink of the second hand furniture to dreams of a life that progresses to some sort of imagined security, some distant heaven on earth.

* * *

A thousand tons of steel lattices covered with zinc sheets enclose the rolling mills . . .Wynn is playin' Black Bitch. He is winning. He unloads the damn Queen on someone else. He understands the principles of the game. He feels good. Later, a lorry comes in, and men start to load it with different qualities and quantities of sheet steel. This is the first lorry they've seen for about three days. They load it inside an hour and go back to playin' cards.

— at the Workin' Man's College awhile back in the utterly beautiful bay, blue, purple, azure, on fire when the sun goes down there was a thumb-sucking twenty three year old blonde with whom the personnel manager — sent for a year's sabbatical — fell in love with despite his wife and three kids. Dolefully, he gazed at her sucking her thumb, and dolefully she gazed back. A year of unfulfilled agony followed. Some fellows get all the luck! Wynn goes to see him just to say hello. The clerk tells Wynn that lover boy is engaged. Wynn goes into obscurity to his flat with the room overhanging the road and to Sybil's embrace.

——0o0——

9

PENDERYN LIMESTONE

> The wage labourer can be neither bought nor sold. What can be bought and sold is his *labour power*;

Wynn puts on his working clothes. Working clothes are clothes that are usually useless; too tight, too loose, holed, ravelled, discoloured, shapeless and dirty. Wynn walked down the road with bacon and egg smothered in lard in his belly his mother had cooked for him O perfect love! He was not alone. He fell in step with other workers, and other school leavers of sixteen years of age. The first thing he did was *clock in*.

The clock was housed under zinc sheets against the quarry office and weighbridge, it was in a little corridor and the workers went in one side of the little corridor and came out the other side of it rather like animals in a market. Wynn put his card, No 44, in the clock and punched it with a handle that protruded from the belly of the clock. Ping! Went the clock. Wynn looked at his card and saw the time printed on it, 7.46, in blue indelible ink. He put the card the other side of the clock in the rack marked IN. Ping! Went the clock. Ping! Ping! As the workers came one by one in the warm summer air to work in the limestone quarry.

Wynn was overwhelmed by the size of the sheds that rose sixty feet in the air. Amazed by their symmetrical form that seemed higgedly piggedly yet somehow beautiful in their silence. Then they growled into life, then whined and were silent: then growled again and finally roared, battered their symbols, stone on stone, metal on stone, metal on metal echoing, echoing in a symphony of noise without melody. And then the thick clouds of dust arose matting his clothes and matting his hair.

And these were the beginning of his quarry days.

Everyday Wynn came home at dinner time. Clocking out and clocking in to eat fish fingers and chips in the council house. But in awhile he felt too tired to walk all that way, besides if you were late they'd dock your money. If you were as much as three minutes late, they'd dock you fifteen minutes off your wages. At that moment he felt humiliated and angry at himself and the system. And began to feel the misery of the proletarian, without knowing its real cause.

At lunch time the quarry shut off the screens, conveyor belts, and crushers while the workers ate their sandwiches in the shacks full of dirt, thick-ribbed limestone dust and cigarette ends. And Wynn joined 'em with his cheese and spam sandwiches, and pickled onions and tea brewed in a can with an oil smear in the water in a spectrum. And the workers ate their food in the silence before the deafening roar of the crushers began. Munch! Munch! Slurp! Slurp! in the silence or gobbin' spittle in the fire from their pipes.

At first Wynn worked in the tar plant. The tar plant coated the stones for the roads. The stones came in different sizes. Wynn's job was to push an iron tram under the hoppers along some iron rails so as to fill it with different size stones to order. He did it with ginger who was from Ystradfellte. Ginger was strong and stubborn and he and Wynn pushed the tram and let the contents into a skip which was then raised by a winch to the height of fifteen feet and tipped into a drier before being coated by tar with the aid of mechanical paddles and dropped into a waiting lorry. And Zoom! they pushed the tram. Bang!

Rattle! it hit the buffers. Whoosh! down went the contents into the skip. Squeak! Squeak! went the skip up fifteen foot. Dust matted their clothing. Dust matted their hair. Noise and cacophony entered their ears. And there was another man there, too, old and feeble who looked after the shute that laid its lip onto the skip and guided the contents of the tram. He closed the shute after the tram was emptied and signalled to the operator upstairs to raise the skip. His name was Arthur.

Arthur told Wynn and Ginger about his erotic adventures
in Merthyr. It was understood that there were loose women in Merthyr. Merthyr had cinemas open on a Sunday. Arthur had false teeth that did n't fit so that when he spoke they fell down and choked off his words. During lapses in activity of filling orders the man and the boys sat around the fire brazier and talked. And in awhile Wynn could see that Arthur was an old fool who was too weak to do his job besides that there was something about Ginger that made Wynn mad.

Ginger was stubborn with the strength of a bullock. He'd push the tram too hard and so they had to stop it and drag it back under the correct chute.

"You push the fuckin' tram too hard," said Wynn.

Ginger looked at him with his freckled face and blue eyes and said nothing in his stubborness. Wind blew through the holes in the zinc sheets, a rag flapped on a stanchion.

"Light the fire, Ginger!" demanded Wynn emphasising the word *ginger* with venom.

Ginger looked at him and said nothing still caught up in his own stubborness. Wynn shaped up like Sugar Ray Robinson. Eye to bloody eye they stood. Wynn in his adolescent rage shut his eyes and struck Ginger in the face. Ginger, in his stone-stubborness and bullock strength, pulled down Wynn's head and thumped his skull.

"Led go you Ginger bastard!" squealed Wynn in the headlock.

Ginger let him go and so Wynn went off to get an oil rag to light the fire from Davy Jones who looked after the boiler rubbing the lump Ginger had raised on his head. SugarRay would've knocked Ginger out, thought Wynn.

And time went by in noise and cacophony.

Davy Jones smoked a pipe over his jaw a bit like Popeye. He always had an oil rag in his hand. Rub! Rub! And an hernia in his scrotum. In other words he had bollux like a bull. Dribble! Dribble went the juice of his pipe down his stubbled, Popeye chin. Never in his life had a drop of alcohol passed his lips except the blood of Christ in the form of a cheap red wine in the chapel opposite his house on the road to Brecon every Sunday O Lord.

"Give us an oil rag for the fire, Mr Jones," said Wynn.

"No fire in the summer, boy," says Davy.

Disgusted, Wynn climbed the tar plant ladder to see Waldo Thomas who mixed the tar. Waldo had a high pitched, almost female, voice who loved his tar-making eerie . . .

— Wynn is carrying Waldo's milk in a churn. It is raining cats and dogs as through the village he goes measuring milk into housewive's jugs; rain dropping off his hat. After, on the road Waldo gives Wynn the price of a packet of fags. Later Wynn goes to the cowshed to smoke one and clear the pungent cow dung up but finds Waldo's village idiot brother in there stood on a stool fuckin' a cow. In/Out: In/Out. Munch! Munch!

responds the cow swinging its tail to and fro. Wynn is amused and disgusted as off he goes through the rain. There's some things you see he thinks that you can never tell your parents about. Much later Waldo is charged with watering the milk. His defence is that the rainwater got in the urn . . .

— Waldo has finished the tar order and is smokin' his navy cut player's fag.

"Hello, Waldo," says Wynn.
"Hello," says Waldo.

"Can I operate the winch on Monday," says Wynn.
Waldo does not reply. All the kids want to operate the winch.

Out of the open window Wynn stares at the hills in the distance and at the trees on the hills. He feels heroic and thinks of tomorrow, of freedom from work, of the pictures in the Aberdare Rex. Funny, he thinks, how Waldo lost the farm. All he had was a couple of cows, and a couple of chickens and that was gone so all he was left with was the tar plant. Too bad. But Waldo was a bit cuckoo, a bit of a twp bloke, however, he did escape being the village idiot. He's left that to his brother.

Wynn climbs down the steel ladder and goes through the buildings and up to the blacksmith's shop and takes a piss in the a bucket outside — urine does something to metal, it hardens it or something. Inside the shop his Uncle Shonni is pounding red hot metal with a hammer. Ping! Bong! Ping! Bong! Ping! His uncle understands the rhythm of metal, and the rhythms of the hammer on metal. He understands the use of the anvil but he does n't understand Wynn. In fact he is training up Dennis Finch, Gobbobimus's brother, to be a blacksmith Shonni's loins has not produced a progeny — when he should be training his nephew . .

— wow! wow! says Shonni to the great Dray horse who's acting up. He slams his fist into the horse's flank and grabs his foot and clamps it between his thighs. The horse neighs but holds still as Shonni jams on the red hot shoe. Hiss! goes the horse's foot as the acrid smoke spirals and wafts into air. Wynn is nine years of age and stands mezmerized at Shonni's antics. Across the Halt he hears the train's whistle blow in the cutting, and the sound of the river comes, too, tinkle! tinkle! in the distance . . .

— he asks Dennis if he's going to the Youth Club and then the work's hooter goes, so Wynn buggers off to get his pay while Dennis and Shonni work overtime on some maintenance project.

When Wynn gets home he gives his mother three pounds for his keep and three pounds for himself. His father thinks Wynn is a great help to the family's finances and calls him his little worker.

Down to the Youth Club goes Wynn. There's art classes. There's drama classes. There's singing classes. There's Mr Price, bald-headed and shining-domed being questioned by kids about the bible — he is a chapel man like Davy Jones. He knows everything there is to know about the bible. Later, Wynn hangs round with Kirsty Morgan who's very hot stuff, and pretty, too. Then, he and Dennis and a few others go to the pub and order glasses of lager with lime. They're under age but what the hell they're all workers. When Wynn gets home he looks in the mirror. He feels good. His eyes shine. No wonder his father's always pissed on Saurday night, he thinks. This lager is pretty good stuff.

As the months go by he's asked to go to the Big Shed. The Big Shed is sixty feet high and houses a type of crusher that transforms small stone to fine dust. Powerful suction pumps suck the dust away through huge pipes that turn and rise into the heights of the shed then dropped into bins below only to be pumped out through a rubber nozzle operated by men, then fed into paper bags weighing 56 to 80 lbs and wheeled into waiting railroad vans. The dust is called Penlim and used to damp down coal mines to stifle escaping gas and to damp down incipient fire.

The men take turns in a rota system so they can operate the nozzle Brrp! Brrp! as the warm dust is worked into the bags to wheel the trolley of up to 120 lbs weight which is designed like a railway porters, or to stack the van.

And time goes by in noise and in cacophony.

Brrp! Brrrp! Ping! Bong! Ping!

Bang! Rattle! Zoom!

Sometimes Wynn goes up to the KB on a gantry set alongside the tram to get the largest stones from the ultimate bin. These stones are crushed down further by a small crusher and returned to the screens. Wynn pokes the mouth of the chute with an iron rod. It is incredibly noisy and its beginning to get cold as time approaches the winter solstice. In awhile he goes down to Dai's boilerhouse to warm up. Davy is there rubbin' his hands with the inevitable oil rag. Rub! Rub! Davy's lookin' at the steam pressure gages on the boiler and unscrews a valve or two. Hiss! Hiss! goes the steam.

Wynn sits down on two railway sleepers used as benches. The place is filthy and smells of steam and oil with draughts blowin' in through the holes in the zinc sheeting. At times men brew tea on Davy's boiler fire, and eat sandwiches there. Suddenly, in bursts the foreman, Buddie Philips, and shouts:

"Get back on that fuckin' KB or you'll be down the road with yo' photos in the window!"

Wynn shit himself.

And scampered back on the KB. It is very dangerous if the bins overload. It could halt the whole process. Buddie Philips is his father's mate. Wynn is learning that life is not a game.

Wynn is doing overtime in the Big Shed on maintenance because he's got a job lookin' after the Drier.

The Drier takes small stones mixed with dust from the bins, it is a huge drum that throws the stones around while a pump blows a diesel flame straight through it. Wynn's job is to look after the conveyor belts and the drum to make sure the aggregate flows evenly and the stone is sufficiently dry to be ground to dust. He seems to get in a bit of trouble here and that is because he does n't do the job properly by talking too much to the men while they're stacking the van and letting the dust stick in the chute. Wynn does n't like the cold and the boredom of watching chutes. Anyhow he is doing overtime on a Sunday with the new foreman of the Big Shed, a very efficient guy with ginger hair. They are up sixty feet looking at one of the pipes which has a hole in it through which the dust leaks like steam. The foreman says:

"Will you be alright if I let you down on a rope to plug that hole."

Wynn is scared out of his wits.

"No," he says.

The foreman says nothing, but starts climbing along the ceiling lattices plugging holes in the roof. The foreman is climbing like a spider, fearless, brave and heroic. Wynn is amazed. This guy is really superior. Wynn's only come across idiots like Waldo and Arthur and Ginger and a lot of other clowns, but this guy is something else. Wynn has got to watch himself or he'll lose his job on the drier. In any case Wynn does n't like overtime because he feels as if he lives in the dirty joint instead of being just a worker. The days seem even longer than before and work continuous in noise filth and cacophony. He begins to feel misery. And thinks of escape.

He goes to pictures a lot. He loves Virginia Mayo, and Debbie Reynolds. He loves Gary Cooper and the Florida Everglades. John Wayne and the deserts of the United States. He loves Oklahoma and Texas. He loves film noir and comedies. In the cinema he watches the clock because of the bus and can never see the end of a film but on weekends he sits through two shows until on Monday he returns to the noise and cacophony of the quarry, to dust and cold and stink of diesel oil.

He needs prestige. He desires to work with clean clothes on, to feel good, to feel a little more important since he is only turned seventeen years of age and his whole life is before him.

Sometimes important people in suits and macintoshes come to look around the quarry. These are senior managers and when they appear the men become obsequious and servile or hide in recesses of the sheds or appear benignly industrious.

Neither is it known exactly where these men come from or what it is they want because the quarry can be completely run by the workers whose sense of responsibility far exceeds the itinerant managers. Wynn keeps his eyes open, and his mouth shut. He is only seventeen years of age. His whole life is before him.

"I'm goin' for a shit," says Wynn.

Going for a shit meant walking to the woods to excrete. This necessity gave relief from the grinding toil and intolerable noise of the crushers. The men shat in the hazel tree copse. There were dollops everywhere covered in blue-bottle flies or wasted and eroded by time and bacteria. Wynn picked his spot and squatted in the green grass. Above him in the trees a crow, startled by his presence, beat his way through the leafy domes to the sky. Krah! Krah! No two men seemed to be in the wood at the same time. They watched and waited and took their turns, and could be seen walking there from the distant, various sheds.

And time went by in noise and cacophony.

And Wynn began to know the fear of coercion. He was scared stiff of Buddie Philips. Buddie Philips had malaria from the war and when he got an attack he began to shake. Buddie had a very bad temper and if anybody crossed him that person would be in very bad trouble. Buddie caught Wynn many times in the lorry drivers' shack watching the drivers playin' nine card don, a game of cards that Wynn did not understand except he was fascinated by the language of the game. The lorry drivers' shack was clean and warm, a little distance away from the tar plant. Wynn had to cross space to get to it. And in the space he was vulnerable. He could get *caught*. Anyway, you could always hide in the spaces and gantries of the sheds, but in the open that was a different thing. So he was always wary about going to the drivers' shack.

Filth, noise, bad hygiene : dreams of the fetid faeces of the wood. Oil. Fumes of creosote and tar nudged the senses toward ! freedom. Wynn went to work in the factory on the plain beneath the mountain above the halt in which he'd been raised. He worked in a plant that made concrete lamp posts and went to work in an old suit on the factory bus where all the people of Penderyn seemed to stare at him. He was now a storeman.

The stores was in an old air raid shelter on the factory estate originally built during the war to make ammunition and so deserted testing ranges were everywhere on the bleak, bogged and bullrushed moorland. The stores was dark and without windows and made of grey concrete and red brick and the lights burned all day as in some film noir thriller. Unlike the quarry it was quiet and there was not much to do.

The problem was the storeman. Initially, he showed Wynn around the stacks where the nuts, bolts and brackets were stored and later he gave Wynn permission to walk around the factory workshop in his old suit. Wynn felt he was some sort of manager, but the feeling passed as quickly as it had come. There was a lot of moulding in concrete going on, and welding, too. The workers worked quickly because they were on piece-work and bonus schemes.

Back in the stores the storeman started to show Wynn some hard core pornography. They were black and white loose photographs he kept wrapped in a brown envelop not taken in a studio but in some council house because of the chintz curtains that were always in the background. They were probably taken in Merthyr or fuckin' Newport, thought Wynn.

The photos were illegal but Wynn liked 'em because they excited him and made his genitals swell and his breath catch. But pornography was a private thing. The sexual feelings they aroused were definately private. But the storeman leaned over him and giggled as he looked at them and Wynn could feel the storeman's sour breath on his cheek. From that moment on

Wynn hated the storeman's guts. He made Wynn's flesh creep and his stupid giggle became intolerable. Every day he was trapped in the cold, damp concrete bunker with the light burning with a man he felt uneasy with and who scared him a little and so he felt he had no option but to quit the job.

When he told the storeman he was quitting the fellow changed the grinning mask became pustulent with hatred and resentment and this was Wynn's experience of homosexual guile and manipulation as a form of seduction but he was hardly aware of it. It was merely an unpleasant and confusing experience. He was only seventeen years of age and had his whole life before him. There were some things you could never tell your parents, he thought.

Wynn went back to work in the quarry except he was now on the railway line maintenance crew. He worked with Fred and a few others. Fred wore his cap straight on his head — most people wore them slanted — and held his trousers up with his belt also he had a waistcoat and a watch. Fred worked like a demon, in absolute concentration, replacing old dogs in the railway sleepers, and tearing out rotten wood between lengths of line, weeding, walking the tracks, weighing trucks at the weighbridge and consulting with Jack Loco.

Bloot! Bloot! went the loco and hiss! hiss! went the steam. And Wynn noticed some men were lazy buggers while others were very industrious who took most of the responsibility. Wynn decided he wanted to be lazy. He liked to observe people and sketch every detail in his mind.

And in his leisure he went to the Youth Club and danced to rock n' roll records and to Frankie Laine and liked to smooch a lot with the girls. He liked to hold their bodies close to his. And went to the pictures and loved all the movies with Virginia Mayo and Doris day and Lana Turner who had lovely blonde hair.

Eventually he got to work on the loco. Bloot! Bloot! He loved Jake 'Loco' Jones. Jake had a red ruddy, chubby face and was broad chested and broken-nosed. Buddie Philips never messed with Jake. And he had pornographic photos or dirty french postcards as they were known, but he never breathed on Wynn's neck when Wynn got a look at 'em like that grinning creep in the factory.

He let you go off to have a look at 'em on your own and Wynn shot his load in his trousers. O stickiness! O aroma of semen! Later, Jake drove the loco up to the quarry to pick up vans and hoppers and pushed and pulled 'em out of little sidings. Chuff! Chuff! Bloot! Bloot! And Wynn uncoupled them with a pole. Clang! Clang! And set the brakes and held the red flag as the loco crossed the road, twice. And jumped back on the loco and rode down the railroad track to Hirwaun and shovelled coal on the fire and pulled the whistle Bloot! Bloot!

One day, as usual, Jack took the loco to get some Penlim vans from the Big Shed, but had to wait awhile for their completion. They often had time to spare in this respect one way or another. Hiss! Hiss! went the engine, and Wynn went over the Davy Jones's boiler to have a warm and a chat when Jack Loco came running out followed by Davy Jones whose pipe fell from his Popeye jaw and whose oil rag sailed through the air at Jack's head together with a tea can.

"Get back on the loco and take that filth with you," yelled an irate Davy whose face had become red as a beetroot and on the floor, under Davy's boots, lay three black and white photographs with the chintz curtains in the background.

And time went by in noise and cacophony.

And one way and another the boys of the quarry were leaving. They had been conscripted into the army, airforce and the navy, and came home in their uniforms from the training camps or disappeared into the far east, into Borneo and Singapore or into the Occupation Zones of Germany.

"Where are you now, then?" Wynn asked Rugby Evans.

"In T . . Tuh . . Tuh . . Tewkesbury," managed Rugby resplendent in his R.E.M.E. uniform. Others sweated it out in the infantry divisions of the South Wales Borderers.

The papers were full of anti-communism, threat and counter threat as wars fermented in the outposts of the lost empire.

"I may be called up," said Wynn's father, "I'm on the Z Reserve."

Wynn's mother made blackberry tart and sniffed into her apron sleeve. The coal fire crackled and a crow alighted in the garden to pick up a bread crust followed by squabbling sparrows.

And time went by in noise and cacophony.

On weekends Wynn went to the papershop in Aberdare run by Mr Davies. It was full of magazines that hung on the wall with newspapers and books set in little wooden compartments that lay flat on the counter. The place smelled of wood and the fragrance of printed paper. And Wynn bought the novels of John O'Hara and Irwin Shaw and went home and read 'em in his bedroom. And his father said:

"What's the bugger doin' now?"

And his mother answered:

"He's in his bedroom reading books."

His father sniffed and gobbed in the fire.

And time went by and people died and were born, and the moon halved and quartered and was once again whole.

"Stop playin' that trombone," said his father, "you're wakin' the neighbors."

"He got a new one today," said his mother, "it came by post from London."

"I hope the bugger's paid for it," opined his father.

And Wynn watched the crows and the sheep and the trout in the river and went to the YMCA dance and kissed a girl under the lamp on the road to the colliery.

"Stop fidllin' with the knobs on that wireless," demanded Wynn's mother.

Bzzz!Whizz!Zonk!Peeow! go the airwaves as Wynn comes across the harmonies and rhythms of jazz. They strike his young heart and his young soul so he goes to Aberdare to get some records He finds the Ken Moule Seven and takes it home and plays it on his portable gramophone over and over.

"Put that bloody noise off," says his father, "I'm tryin' to sleep."

Soon its Benny Goodman, Duke Ellington, and Louis

Armstrong.

"That bugger can't sing ," said his father.

And time goes by as before in noise and cacophony. Bloot! Bloot!Chuff! Chuff! goes the loco until one day Wynn gets his call-up papers and goes to report to Frederick street in Cardiff.

"Eat plenty of sweets and piss in the b . . b . . buh . . bottle," says Rugby on leave again to see his schoolgirl sweetheart, "and they'll put you down for too much sugar."

It was November 1956 and the frost was on the ground. The quarry looked quiet in the distance. The trees had shed their leaves. The crows were around, forlorn and desolate in the fields awaiting another winter. His mother sat beside the fire and watched the flames dance.

"Got your razor, towel and toothpaste?" asked his father, and, as an after-thought, continued, "you can have my shaving brush."

That night when the darkness came down Wynn lay in an RAF billet in Cardington, Bedfordshire. It was bledy freezin'. Having slept little with the cold he went into the toilets and shaved with the aid of his father's shaving brush. Goose pimples came up on his arms and chest as he shivered uncontrollably. Fuck this, he thought, which was an idea shared by twenty or more other souls in the toilets as they, too, shivered and blasphemed.

And time went by as before in noise and cacophony.

*   *   *

And so its goodbye. Goodbye to the quarry years. Goodbye Davy Jones and your oil rag. Goodbye Jack Loco. Bloot! Bloot! Goodbye Waldo! Goodbye Buddie Philips! Goodbye Gerald! Goodbye Arthur who told us erotic stories of Merthyr Tydfil. Goodbye Bang! Rattle! Zoom! Rub! Rub! Goodbye Dribble! Goodbye In out/In out! Ping Bong! Ping Bong! Goodbye Uncle Shonni. (Wow! Wow!) & Brrp! Brrp! Chuff! Chuff! Goodbye days of rain and sunshine and dust in the spaces and the gantries of the quarry.

GOODBYE

———0o0———

10

THE RECRUIT

The December mist came across from the Mersey onto RAF West Kirby, a boot training camp. Wynn dumped his kit on the bed. He had a high temperature like 103 and a cough with a pain in his left rib cage near the sternum.

He says to the corporal:

"I feel sick." The corporal shouts: "STAND TO ATTENTION WHEN YOU'RE TALKIN' TO ME, AIRMAN!

Wyn's head seems to burst like a shell Boom! Boom! His eyes water. He coughs and the pain shoots into his ribs. "REPORT SICK ACROSS THE SQUARE: LEFT RIGHT/LEFT RIGHT Et cetera . ."

Wynn staggers across the square to the sick bay : a nurse puts a thermometer in his mouth, and finds him a bed. He is delirious and plaqued by hallucinations, and fever. He is only eighteen and has his whole life in front of him. The medics pump penicillin up his ass, (his mother pronounces pennyshillin') boom! boom! And the fever subsides except his chest is full of mucuous. Cough! Cough! Later Wynn goes in for an x-ray. They push a tube into his trachea Pop! and pump some fluid into his lungs. His ribs go numb. Much later a physio comes round and pummels his chest slam! bang! boff! so Wynn coughs up the shit they've pumped into him.

Unlike the billets the hospital is warm as toast. Wynn feigns discomfort and is sent home for Christmas. At Aberdare station a youth shouts at him across the street. He is embarrassed in his RAF uniform and stands paralysed to the spot. British Rail does n't even ask him for his ticket. He feels heroic and miserable at once. In Penderyn all the boys come to see him, Gobbobimus, Rugby Evans, and Dennis among others. And off he goes down the Youth Club with them, but things seem to have changed. The girls seem more interested in him.

Kirsty Morgan holds his hand and leads him down the dark lane but stops under the lamp so he does n't get to start any nonsense. He makes a grab for her buttocks. "Ooo," she says, "you 'ave changed." And rubs his cock. And "com'on," she says, "I got to catch the bus." After she's gone he goes to the pub and drinks two pints. "It's bledy tough in the RAF," he says to Gobbobimus, "the corporals are cunts."

Later, his father comes home from Liverpool in a huff, dressed in a pinstriped suit with a cap and white muffler, puffin' a Woodbine.

"They never told me you was comin' home," he said, "they gave me a bed in the hospital, though."

And Wynn went back to the boot camp with his trombone. He'd heard the band flight was a doddle. However, when he woke up in the morning a lot of airmen were shadow boxin' and runnin' round the block with their shorts on in the freezin' rain.

"Get up an' run round the block," said the billet leader.

"What's this, then?" asked Wynn.

"It's the sport's flight," said the billet leader.

"Fuck it," said Wynn, "I just come out of hospital, and I'm sick. I'm supposed to be in the band flight."

The billet leader buggered off over the ashes the flight corporal had thrown all over the oil-cloth so the recruits could work their asses off cleanin' it up spick an' span.

In the next couple of days Wynn was sent to the band flight after passing a test in which the band sergeant gave him a piece to read and then waved his arms. Wynn blew a few notes out of rhythm and out of tempo and that's how he got in the band flight. One day they were all learning marches for the parade when the band sergeant stopped the band and told the hubbly-bubblies to shaddup. The hubbly-bubblies were the saxophones. Wynn noticed that the saxophonists all posed as jazz musicians which got on the sergeant's nerves cause they could n't play anyway and that's why he called saxophones hubbly-bubblies.

Well, if it did n't do anything else the airforce instilled some rhythm into Wynn. "Left/Right a-bout turn . . 1234. Lift your feet up you dull prick! Don't you know your left from your right, airman? Left/Right: Left/Right"

In a while Wynn started to enjoy the drills, and the drill corporal was OK. He had a room at the end of the billet, and sometimes Wynn brought the drunken oaf a mug of tea on Sunday mornings. It was then noticed the sordid life the corporal was livin' and he sensed his loneliness hunched there under the bedclothes. It was n't a pleasant idea at all.

One day Wynn asked one of the bandsman about religion. The bloke was a Salvation Army member. He knelt down beside Wynn's bed and told him about God and Jesus, but Wynn was embrrassed because the bloke had a pious look on his mug like he was in love with a real dame with breasts and a great ass instead of some abstraction in the sky. He never asked the bloke about religion again, but these salvation army blokes were good musicians because they had training in a brass band in love with God unlike the saxophonists who were only in love with themselves.

And the days went by to the beat of the big base drum.

Now the band flight had white webbin', and a badge on the arm in the shape of an aeolian harp. One day the bandsmen were all sitting around the iron stove spitting on boot toe-caps and making circular movements so as to shine 'em like mirrors. This was "called bullin' the boots." Some had the knack of makin' the boots shine while others did n't.

"How d'you do it then?"

"I just spit and polish. Spit and polish."

"Oh, yeah! God! Well, I can't do it."

"Too much polish, Taffy, an' not enough spit, an' wider circles to begin with."

"I'll give you a packet of fags if you do mine . ."

And everybody lapsed into silence around the stove spittin' an' polishin'. Then someone had a bright thought.

"Let's put on white webbin' belts and make out we're red caps."

"Yeah, a bloomin' good idea."

They put on their great coats and white webbin' belts and shining boots, well, some shinin' boots, and paraded down the middle of the billet. The recruits froze. Wynn savoured the moment of absolute power, struttin' like a peacock. One recruit sat on his bed. Wynn strutted up.

"Name! Number! Rank!" he screamed

The airman stood up rigid and spat out his identity like the rhythm of a bren gun.

"Clean up this barrack, airman!"

And he turned and strutted down the corridor between the beds like a king or some tin-pot dictator in a banana republic.

"We'll 'be back," said *another* phoney red-cap.

Outside it was dark and the late Autumn wind rose

bearing a winter chill on its back. Above the moon scudded between cumulus clouds.

"That was bledy great," said a voice out of a Yorkshire Brass Band set in some mining town.

Later the recruits found out it was the band flight that had humiliated them, and they came into the billet in a murderous pale-faced mood, threatening their tormentors. Everyone went silent, polishing their boots beside the stove.

And the days went by to the beat of the big bass drum.

After square-bashing, a bout of pneumonia, and adventures with the band flight the world's worse trombonist, without rhythm, without pitch, and therefore without form, was dispatched to Spitalgate, Nr Lincoln, England, to train as a batman/waiter for the officer class.

The barracks consisted of two-story concrete buildings with central heating. Such bliss! Such worldliness! It was here Wynn took his father's shaving brush and tossed it out of the window, an act he would remember all his life, though the reason for this symbolic act was not yet known.

The batman/waiter's course consisted of learning how to lay tables for the officer's mess from soup to the dessert, how to press trousers, how to remove stains from clothing, and lay out ceremonial dress ready for banquets.

Wynn passed with 74% answering questions from a po-faced warrant dfficer with pock marks on his puss. This is really pansy stuff for a bloke who's unloaded 16 tons of coal in a morning with Fred on the quarry line. A resentment starts to build up. Going home one day he meets a bloke from Cefn Coed Grammar School who's working in the records department at

Barnwood, Gloucester. He gives the bloke his service number. Wallop! He's posted to RAF Innsworth, Gloucester, a spit of a distance to the South Wales Coal Field and his ol' man performing surplus value for the. NCB.

RAF Innsworth is a transition camp where airman come to be demobbed from the Far East and other places. Wynn works in the officer's mess, layin' the tables, making melba toast, brewin' coffee, and makin' tea served in silver pots. He's full of *resentment*, works slowly, reluctantly, but the food's good so what the 'ell. One day a little ginger runt picks a fight with him. They go outside. He uses his left. Smack! It hits the guy in mouth ; the fight's over. In comes a corporal in his thirties who runs the officer's mess bar. The fellow wants to take Wynn apart and he's very excited, his eye-pupils are dilated with adrenalin, he's got a buzz on. He faces up to Wynn but he's a little scared of the left jab maybe. Anyhow he threatens Wynn and buzzes off back in the bar. Wynn reckons he can handle anybody in a fight.

Wynn's sleepin' quarters are in an officers billet. The officers, unlike the enlisted men, sleep in their own rooms and it is Wynn's job to wake 'em up after placing their polished shoes outside their doors. The sweet-sour human smell greeted him as he went into their small bedrooms. Most of 'em were deep in sleep when he entered : and this is the way he was taught to raise 'em - gently tug the pillow until they awake piss-proud and sticky-eyed. He hated the fuckers. They lived like kings served by the proletariat who they looked down on, or, were totally indifferent to.

One of 'em was an especially arrogant pig with a flat red-ruddy face and piercing blue eyes. Unlike the others he was always awake and in his dressing gown complaining about his shoes or his tea, or wanting his trousers pressed. In awhile Wynn got to thinking the bloke was tryin' to communicate somehow with the lower orders in his own inimitable way. What did it all mean? Anyhow, the officers were always complainin' about the batmen.

"They be watchin' yow," said Wynn's companion from the Forest of Dean who was always tryin' to wrestle. He was very intense tryin' to be tough. Wynn never resisted him much in their wrestling matches.

"Give in," opined the bloke.

Wynn gave in.What was the point? The situation would have really got nasty if he had n't.

And the days went by to the hiss of steam, and the rattle of cutlery, to the gurgle of white wine and fish, to the crunch of melba toast and the slurp of soup: to resentment in the blood, pique, huff and petty tiffs.

One day Wynn was removed from the dining hall and told to mow the lawn outside the mess and weed the rose beds. After he'd finished he sat on the steps. Out came the civilian mess manager and asked him why he was sitting there. Wynn said he'd finished the job. The manager looked at Wynn with distain. Next day he was transferred to Barnwood officer's mess. A little joint. All this movin' about got on Wynn's nerves. All he could think of was getting out and back to his council house and his warm bed overlookin' the woods. Every other sonofabitch in this service life was a pig. Every other sonofabitch tried to do you some harm.

They did n't like the way you walked, or the way you looked. They did n't like your attitude or where you came from. Besides you lived like some animal, sleepin' in beds lined up as in some salvation army doss house. The billet in Barnwood was made of concrete slabs with the usual stove. Eveyone in their billet was talking about a red-haired Irishman who was terrorizin' them.A couple of weeks later Wynn brought back his trombone, a cheap model in a cardboard-thin case — he'd heard someone was startin' a jazzband . . . O Kid Ory! O Jack Teagarden! O Miff Mole! ET CETERA. But the project came to nuthin' as usual. After the session he had his trombone on his bed when in came our camp bully, the red-haired Irishman stinkin' of beer and whisky.

"Whad you got in the fuck'n' case!" he demanded.

"A trombone," said Wynn, his knees like jelly, really scared.

"Let's fuck'n' look at it," said the man.

But Wynn would n't let anyone look at his trombone in case they wanted to blow it an' that led to all sorts of problems like droppin' the slide an' things.

"No," he said.

With that the Irish camp bully took Wyn by the lapels and rammed him hard against the locker boom! Wynn could smell the fumes of alcohol emanating from the bloke's mug and his legs turned to more jelly. He was scared and then fright turned to fight and an anger rose in him, but suddenly bully boy let him go.

"Where'd yuh come from, Taff ?" he asked.

"Innsworth to work in the officer's mess," he answered, his mouth dry, and his arms heavy and stiff.

"Just watch it in future," said our ginger man and went away.

Watch what? thought Wynn, I have n't done nutnin'. Fuggin' typical of this set-up. Watch this! Watch that! Move there! Bull this! Bull that! Drunks comin' in the billets waking you up, threatenin' you, people markin' off days on the calender like they were in some sort of prison. Fellows sayin' "that's it I'm finished!" wavin' clearance cards and for what? To face up to those bolshi Russians. O, yeah, the communists. What did we have against 'em anyhow? Hywel Williams of the Pandy Lodge was a communist who checked his father's pay to see if he was diddled by the management. What's so bad about that?

The Germans were the enemy. We occupied the Germans. But the communists were the new enemy facing up in Berlin which was in sectors. The Russians were facin' up to the Americans. The Russians were bad guys and the Americans good guys. The communists were inspired by Russians and were always makin' trouble in factories an' that. Only the Americans did not have communists except for some spies, but the Russians did. Wynn could n't think of anything the Russians were good at except ballet whereas the Americans had Louis Armstrong, Count Basie and Duke Ellington together with Doris Day. Later, after thinkin' about all this he fell asleep on his bed, exhausted.

And time went by as before.

The officer lay back in his chair like a king. He said: "there's a new regime around here, and there's goin' to be some changes made." The officer lay back in his chair with his campaign ribbons and his garbardine uniform while Wynn stood before him in his thick, coarse flannels, ill fitting and baggy with his neck being chaffed by an equally ill fitting collar and stud. The officer lay back and said : "and get your haircut and polish your badge for god's sake,"

A couple of days later the same officer was yelling about the coffee, the toast, and the fried eggs when Wynn lost his marbles and threw the coffee and the eggs on the mess floor splash! slurp!. “Fuck you and your regime,” he yelled back with tears of frustration in his eyes.

“Put yourself under arrest,” said the officer in a state of shock at being talked back to, and Wynn marched down to the guard room and said to the fat Indian MP. “The officer told me to put myself under arrest.” But the Indian replied that he’d never heard of an airman putting himself under arrest. He then made a phone call to the mess. And the outcome was this: Wynn was transferred back to Innsworth to the airman’s mess.

He lay in bed smokin’ four days without being accounted for. Smokin’, dreamin’, eatin’ three meals a day, watchin’ the cooks comin’ an’ goin’. Smokin’, dreamin’, warmin’ himself beside the stove, goin’ down the NAAFI an’ eatin’ doughnuts with hot tea. Smokin’ dreamin’ of Penderyn, of his room and the boiler gurglin’ with the smell of clean sheets, dreamin’ of peace and solitude. Dreamin’ of takin’ the perfect trombone solo.

In awhile he presented himself to the mess and was told to report to the tin room. By lunchtime he was clothed in denims up to his neck in tins, or trays stinkin’ of cooked meat and fish, up to his neck in stewin’ pots, custard pots, or remnants of rice puddin’. Woosh! Splosh! Rub and Scrub! That’s how it went. Water everywhere. What the ’ell . . . you did n’t have to think, nor worry about some garbardine-clad megalomaniac officer just rub and scrub an’ think about home, an’ dream.

He noticed that airman’s billets were n’t that bad considering those concrete slabs at Barnwood, then one night in came another bully an’ rammed him against the locker, stinkin’ of alcohol, the bloke’s mug an inch from his like a gargoyle from hell, breathing hell’s noxious fumes. What kind of life was this?

Nineteen years of age and the butt of everyone's ire. A proletarian's life.

Wynn was in the Cotswolds an area of exquisite beauty with idyllic sandstone cottages and pubs situated in little wooded dells and valleys. He was outside a pub playin' slow tunes from *Oklahoma*. He'd learned to fake the arrangments by playin' one note rhythms by ear. Oompa! pa! pa! Oompa pa! pa! pa! . . . (rest) . . pa! ETC This is the life, a bandsman's life. Out came the beer from the pub oom! blurp! Oom blurp! This is the life . .

"What's this," asked the sergeant, some cretin, a seventy two hour pass to play with the band !??* get back in that room, airman !??* "

Wynn lay on the floor of the bus shelter. He'd had too much to drink. His stomach had given way, a very nervous stomach. He lay in the cigarette-stumped, urine-sodden bus shelter outside Gloucester somewhere paralysed in his own vomit, shivering, unable to move. A cop came from nowhere.

" 'What's the matter," asked the cop.

"Too much to drink! Sick! Ow! Oo!"

Next thing Wynn's in the guard house watchin' the little light in the ceiling. Later, its Left Right/Left Right under close arrest down the mess for breakfast. Greasy bacon and greasy eggs. Vomits on the green outside. Back to the guard house. Left Right/Left Right: squad halt! And the outcome?

Seven days jankers from some twat officer sitting behind a desk. More tins. More toilets, more polishin', spittin'.Loses job in tin room : is now on supply truck with civilian taking supplies from main-stores to the messes, goes homewith suitcase full of pork chops.

"Christ," says his father, "he's a man of the world now with all those pork chops."

And time goes by in hope for the future, for release from polishin' buttons, washin' dishes, scrubin' tins an' stealin' pork chops.

Sometime he goes to a dance down the YMCA in Hirwaun. Lovely girls down there. The place smells of perfume, ironed dresses, brillcreem, and brilliantine. Johnny 'Cry' Ray is beltin' out famous tunes and so is Frankie Laine. Wynn goes to the toilet. Bubble! Bubble!

There's a couple of blokes loitering in there, a ginger bloke with a stupid look on his face, and a dark good lookin' bloke. Wynn takes a piss. Bubble! Bubble! goes the toilet. When Wynn tries to leave the toilet the dark good lookin' boy bars his way at the door. Wynn looks at him and says:

"If you don't open the door, I'll smash your face in," just like that, real tough. The fellow then opens the door, but slams it on Wynn's ankle when he leaves. Bollux . He's made his point. Real tough guy. Wynn goes down to the hall and does some dancin'. The girls smell lovely. Their bodies are warm and soft. He's in the forces. He's a hero. He's tough. Soon it's time to go. In the foyer of the YMCA the good lookin' kid is sitting on the table where they took tickets earlier in the evening. He says:

"You said you'd smash my face in."

Wynn is really annoyed. This fucker is lookin' for trouble.

"Come outside, just you an' me," says Wynn, a real tough guy. He can take on anybody with his left jab. They go outside. Wynn shapes up like Sugar Ray. "Not here," says the fellow, "there might be police." for some reason they walk toward the colliery. Drab clouds are in the sky. The good lookin' fellow starts to talk, nervously. Wynn says, real tough, "shaddup, we've come here to fight." He's got in mind some kind of boxin' match like Madison Square Garden.

It starts to rain. They stand under the eaves of a cottage. Wynn looks up toward the colliery when BANG! the fellow hits him right on the chin, lights flash in his skull as his brain rocks in its fluid and his teeth bite down on his tongue, lacerating it. He is stunned but turns on his tormentor and pitches two short hooks to the head. He's so close he brings his knee into the bloke's groin. The fellow is strong, he takes Wynn by the lapels and smashes his head against the wall of the house bomp! Oh god! and the strength leaves his body as he slips to the hard ground. Then the guy kicks him in the stomach for good measure. Suddenly someone runs from the cottage and shouts CLEAR OFF! and the good lookin' fellow runs. Inside the cottage Wynn's surrounded by people who ask him if he's OK. But he's concussed. There's a curtain between the objective world and his mind. He feels distant, odd, exhausted. In awhile his tormentor appears in the doorway. "Is he alright?" he asks. "Clear off!" repeats the man, a railway worker of sorts, still clad in his trousers and regulation waistcoat.

John Jones walks Wynn halfway to Penderyn. Wynn's father is really disturbed when he gets home. "Who did it!" he asks. Wynn won't tell him. He turns to restless sleep, shocked, with a sickening headache, his tongue sore and swollen, his shoulder and neck in pain. He has let his father down, and himself. He feels the burden of shame.

And time goes by as before with murderous intent in the lacerated sky where the moon bleeds and crows are born on the black side of the sun.

Back in the camp the boys tell him to keep out of trouble cause he can't fight, anyhow, and never turn your back on anybody. And the bloke did n't know his good luck when Wynn turned up to take his title. In awhile Wynn's had enough of RAF Innsworth and the meat wagon and volunteers for service overseas. Might as well see as much as you can at the government's expense.

He remembers nothing of leaving Innsworth. Easy come. Easy go. He lays on the bunk of the troop ship. Clank! Clank! goes the ship's engines. Wynn falls asleep. He wakes at dawn, cold in the summer's morning. Long, dark green carriages are lined up on the docklands of the Hook of Holland, bigger and more powerfull than their British counterparts.

And time went by as before in all its complexity, in human consciousness *a priori*, in dreams, in nuances of light and shade, in the flowers and in the leaves of trees.

———0o0———

In training.

The author on trumpet amongst manuscripts.

The author on trumpet.

A painting done by the author while proof-reading this book.

"This is a social club not a den of iniquity. In here we play dominoes and chequers. It's a joint for the working Blackman, not a house for pimps and petty thieves, and there's no Mahilia Jacksons, no Sammy Davies Jnrs, nor Nat King Coles or Chubby Chequers: no Ella Fitzgeralds, Billie Holidays and no niggers. They're called Mohammed, Harry, Abdullah, George, Arthur and Tom. Nobody plays the guitar, saxophone, or trumpet. And we don't smoke pot or sniff cocaine. So, unless you wanna play dominoes or cribbage take a hike and watch the sun go down."

* * *

Yank thought life was getting far too complicated. Why don't people just get high and open up their minds to the experience, to see the new world where there is no anxiety, where there was only PEACE OF MIND? And through the channels of his ear came "Lucy in the Sky with Diamonds" and "Bridge over Troubled Waters" as the fever of hepatitis B started to subside.

* * *

He was in the Double Deuce having a Southern Comfort the Wop had given him in a fit of tenement generosity when a stranger came up and started to talk to him.

The Yank listened.

"I won the lottery mate, me an' the missus, well, she wasn't really my missus just livin' together, like. We bought our dream home and we had a car, one each, actually, an' then, well, everything fell apart. Nuthin' to do, mate. My missus gave up her job 'cause all the of fice workers started callin' her flashy Jane an' she missed her lunch hour in the pub an' all the office gossip and then she started doin' DIY in the house changin' all the colours all the time, drove me bledy mad: and then I had nuthin' to do but go down the race track and lose my money and so, well, we split up 'cause, basically, we had nuthin' to do . . . we got a little kid an', well, I live with my parents now and so does she, well, we might get back together, but bledy money isn't everything, mate, it can ruin your bledy life, like, I mean . ."

"You wouldn't like to invest in a theatrical agency?" opinioned the Yank. "WHAT! YOU FLICKERS ARE THE SAME. AFTER A FAST BUCK."

And the Yank fled into the loo and took two valium to calm down. If the Wop knew he was drawin' attention to himself by puttin' the arm on a customer he would be in real big trouble: it simply was against the house rules and what with the Wop's temper . . . well. Anyway, the guy was a nutter, anyone could see that. And the Yank sat on the loo for half an hour tryin' to forget the whole thing.

Outside the sun when round the heavens as before and the shadows lengthened along the streets, under the eaves of the houses of the town, under the trees on the avenues. And a wind rose and the sea got a little choppier while women walked the streets coughing into their handkerchiefs and dogs did their business on the pavements despite the warnings of the local council, and a shopkeeper hung himself in a garage because he couldn't meet the mortgage payments.

* * *

Night. The Yank went down the Chinese restaurant with two goons. They sat deep inside, near the bar and ordered a meal. Halfway through the meal the two goons got up and knocked the rice, the noodles and the bean pancakes all over the floor. "Dis flickin' food is no good," said one, "we want chips instead, fish 'n' flickin' chips with ketchup and pickles."

"But, sirs," protested the Chinese manager, "this is a Chinese restaurant with the best Chinese cuisine. We have won prizes. We have certificates in hygiene."

"We don't care. We're British an' we want fish 'n' flickin' chips or else."

The Yank, who was sitting at another table, minding his own business said: "Excuse me, but I can't help overhearing this dispute and I think . . ."

"We don't care what you think you pock-marked little ginger punk!" And a goon pushed him backward against a table over which the Yank fell knocking a family's best Chinese cuisine meal all over their laps. Kerplunk!

From the back of the restaurant came two Chinese cooks with meat cleavers while one of the goons produced an army revolver, saying:

"If you gooks make one more move I'm gonna blow your inscrutable mugs into next week."

All froze.

"We'll be back for our fish 'n' flickin' chips, don' worry. We're British."

Among the sounds of profound apologies and promises of free Chinese meals and dry cleaning bills the goons left followed closely by the Yank and many appalled customers.

Later, in the week, a tall man would show up with a hooked nose and receding hair smelling of cheap deodorant, mouth wash and cat litter commingled with sour body odour to ask for the Chinese manager and on explaining about the trouble a couple of days before would like to reassure his honourable oriental friend that such a row would never occur again. He then produced a card which read:

PROTECTION RAQUETEERS
Komedy Klub
(An entertainment forum)
Tel: 07710 321000

"And I wouldn't phone the police if I were you, sir, because they're too busy to deal with this kind of thing what with all the traffic accidents and the muggin's and the white collar crime that goes on together with child molesters etcetera, and, I would like to assure you that your business from this time on will prosper provided you pay a little contribution from the takings to the Komedy Klub which is, after all, a well known charity."

Later, the Chinese phoned the number which was of a mountain telephone booth in the middle of nowhere and from a car parked nearby came a shadowy figure in a mac pulling up his collar against the rain. The Chinese was told to pay ten per cent of his takings in cash to the pock-faced little punk with a white rose in his lapel after, of course, he had been given a free meal without sweet and sour sauce because it upsets his little sensitive British stomach.

Far out at sea a boat was bobbin' in the tides with a load of lobsters, and a light kept flashing from it as though it was in distress. The lobsters were a little heavy not with white succulent meat, but a kind of brown resin. After a while it proceeded in toward the land, into a little bay called smuggler's cove where in the caves were still the remnants of some old brandy barrels lulling to and fro in the trapped spaces, as though echoing dastardly deeds of long ago.

* * *

How the Yank got it in his mind that the spades were dope fiends he didn't know. Too much propaganda, he thought, too many ideas comin' from books and stories about jazz musicians in the Reader's Digest. Did they really call themselves Mississippi an' ebony an' all that or was it some kind of dream. Another thing: was the Wop really a gangster, and was he himself a gangster's hoodlum, though he preferred the word lieutenant? It had more class about it. Was his brain too addled with heroin, cocaine, cannabis, downers, uppers, speed, and codeine? It was all a mix-up. Oh, why weren't things more simple as they were in the sixties when all his generation wanted was LOVE. Maybe I'm too ambitious, he thought, ambition which leaps o'er itself and falls on the other side. Ambition was 'orrible: ambition which had crept up on him and had began to torment him. Oh, Lady Macbeth of the Soul! Ambition the Two Backed Monster was eating away at his Peace of Mind.

* * *

"You won't get far with McCluskey you won't, you stink, you do, of cats and you never take a bath. You're just like those cats you got: hate water."

"Mind your business you Junkie little Yank with your white socks and black slip-on shoes!" sniffed the Spiv.

"Don't you call me a junkie! You need a good meal you do if you ask me."

"Nobody's askin' you."

"You started it."

"No, I didn't."

"Yes, you did,"

"If the Wop finds out he'll never promote you."

"If he finds out you keep callin' him a Wop you'll end up in concrete boots."

"Stupid ass. The water's too shallow in this little sea here. I'd be standin' up like a lead soldier for everybody to see."

"He'll bump you off one of these days, Spiv."

"Him, and whose army!"

"Really tough you are, Spiv, when he ain't even here, and when he is here you're like a church mouse tremblin' an' twitchin', lookin' for some hole to crawl in."

"And you, all you do is hide in the toilet and take a fix o'junk."

"Shaddup!"

"You shaddup! You're yellow."

"I'm not yellow, you are."

"Stupid ass. I don't mean that kind of yellow. I mean liver-yellow. Hepatitis back is it — the junkies' dilemma, eh?"

"At least I'm not fee-faw-fum."

"What?"

"Afraid of the bugaboo, burnin' lights all night in that bedsit of yours an' stealin' ouda the Wop's till for the electric meter."

"Shaddup!"

"You shaddup!"

And through the air condition ducts the sound of two plaintive voices argued into the night and wafted over the polluted sand of the beach and the little waves that slapped, feebly, on oil sodden bay. And the voices dissolved in the sound of the sea, dissolved to nothing but salty air and salt spray and moonlight.

*   *   *

Up went the Yank to his council flat on the hill overlooking the sea, shivering from his fever and in a while he stopped to vomit in the hedgerow, wondering if his giro cheque had come 'cause the Wop had not paid him again. Anyhow, he told his wife it was only a trial job and he expected to be taken on full time soon when he passed his probation. In any case he was all set up for free meals in the Chinese so things were lookin' up a bit. Over the sea down came the moonlight through a cloud and he thought he saw some angels descending over the Double Deuce and he took it as a sign that everything would turn out all right and he would be given the post of entertainments manager and maybe one day run his own theatrical agency. Meanwhile, he'd take a fix of horse the Wop had given him and all the night's anxiety would go away. Yeah, everything was workin' out ok. Tomorrow was, after all, another day when hope would spring eternal and he, the Yank, would go down that road which Antonio McCluskey had opened for him, a road of opportunity with a pot of gold at the end if he played his cards right.

And the wind rose again and the clouds closed the ladder of moonlight over the sea and it started to rain ever so slightly sending a chill through his body and he began to sweat and feel faint and he stopped and closed his eyes and took a deep breath and an animal cried out in distress and a fox barked somewhere and a light went on in a house and then off again and he opened his eyes and a pain started in his side like a stitch and he wanted to vomit again and his legs went weak and then it all passed and he felt tranquil and he started up the hill again toward home and rest and some comfort and at least he had a home unlike the Spiv who had nuthin' except those stinkin' cats, yeah, tomorrow was another day and there was parent's evening and the kid who was doin' so well with her exams unlike me who had blown it all with my first fix all those years ago to kill anxiety and had made me into a junkie and that's what I am, a junkie . . . the die had been cast and the mould could not be broken . . . a junkie but what the 'ell was wrong with that . . . nuthin' as far as he knew . . . he was a human being like everybody else.

"Where've you bin?" demanded his wife, "you look dreadful. There's some bubble and squeak on the table and a glass of beer in the fridge and don't make a noise when you come to bed in case you wake your daughter. And if you hang about that bledy club anymore I'll knock your bledy block off. You'll find a brand new sterilized needle in the bathroom and a tourniquet. I'm gonna sleep now 'cause I got to get up early in the morning for the toy factory."

Over the windowsill blew the wind and there came the sound of raindrops against the glass as the temperature suddenly dropped and some unseasonable snowflakes cut a pattern in the night air resting on the privet hedges and swallowed by the unrelenting cold eddies of the eternal sea far below in the bay Yank Williams had left behind, that is, until tomorrow.

REVELATION

Solitude. Rest. Contemplation on the farm.
He saw stars go round the universal sky,
far from the city's crowds, far from harm
where truth masquerades as lie.

This man saw a benign God eye to eye
in the timeless firmament,
and he saw Him there with a bit of style
in a dream of heavenly contentment.

Now he sits in the corner old and wise,
with cataracts growing in his eyes.

OLD SOLDIER

Wash his mouth with glycerine!
(Two lovely nurses in the team.)
Sputum and fuzz cake on his ageing tongue:
No teeth either protrude from his gum.

Any message he wishes to convey is in his face
where shells implode
on a long, wet, evening road
somewhere in a forgotten land, a forgotten place.

NOTES

The world described in the pages of this black comedy no longer exists. It has now drifted, inexorably, into history. The flames of revolution have dampened in the rainstorms of time and drift, like smoke, into the air.

1.1 The means of production remains secure in the hands of capitalists, *clause four* having been abandoned by New Labour under Tony "Third Way" Blair.

1.2 The Soviet Union collapsed. The barbed wire and watch towers of Europe that stretched from the Baltic to the Adriatic torn down and Germany re-united.

1.3 National Service abandoned. The inflationary demands of unions shackled by Tory legislation under Margaret "Handbag" Thatcher who played her part with Gorbachev in dismantling communism.

1.4 In this world there were hardly any household telephones only public boxes made of wrought iron and painted red, now collector's pieces. TV's were black and white, and constantly malfunctioned. There were no computers, no internet, no mobile phones, and no credit cards. People read books and went around with Dylan Thoms in their pockets.

1.5 The only celebrities were trades union bosses, and fat lady politicians like Bessie Braddock, and red shop stewards from the car factories of Birmingham. All gone into the smoke of history.

1.6 The psychiatric hospitals are gone forever. The train lines through the valleys and coastal plains shut. Bloot! Bloot! Doctors smoked Players and died of lung cancer and the coal miner smoked Woodbines and died of cancer. If you did not smoke you were not a man.

1.7 What's left of feminism is the lingering legislation of domestic abuse now a crime, equal opportunities, and divorce laws. Women remain women and men remain men. All walk streets under the sun and under the moon's glow.

GOODBYE WORLD